IRÈNE NÉMIROVSKY

Jezebel

·····················

Irène Némirovsky was born in Kiev in 1903 into a wealthy banking family and immigrated to France during the Russian Revolution. After attending the Sorbonne in Paris, she began to write and swiftly achieved success with *David Golder,* which was followed by more than a dozen other books. Throughout her lifetime she published widely in French newspapers and literary journals. She died in Auschwitz in 1942. More than sixty years later, *Suite Française* was published posthumously for the first time in 2006.

VINTAGE

INTERNATIONAL

IRÈNE NÉMIROVSKY

Jezebel

TRANSLATED FROM THE FRENCH BY
Sandra Smith

························

·VINTAGE INTERNATIONAL·
Vintage Books
A Division of Random House, Inc.
New York

A VINTAGE INTERNATIONAL ORIGINAL, MAY 2012

Translation copyright © 2010 by Sandra Smith

Library of Congress Cataloging-in-Publication Data
Némirovsky, Irène, 1903–1942.
[Jézabel. English]
Jezebel / Irène Némirovsky ; translated from the French by Sandra
Smith.
p. cm.
ISBN 978-0-307-74546-0 (trade pbk.)
1. Trials (Murder)—France—Fiction. I. Smith, Sandra. II. Title.
PQ2627.E4J4913 2012
843'.912—dc23
2012000607

www.vintagebooks.com

Printed in the United States of America
10   9   8   7   6   5   4   3   2   1

Introduction

A woman takes the stand, accused of murdering her young lover. A succession of witnesses are called to testify to her character. Gladys Eysenach listens in silence, admitting to the crime but refusing to explain why she has committed murder.

'Jezebel' . . . the very name immediately conjures up a host of impressions, all negative: seductress, traitor, whore. Yet the Jezebel of the Old Testament was not originally condemned for her loose morals, but for convincing her husband, King Ahab, to reject the God of Israel in order to worship the Phoenician god, Baal. Némirovsky's Jezebel worships an idol as well: her own beauty. To her, beauty is power; it defines her life and her worth. As Gladys ages and her fears turn to obsessions, Némirovsky explores the fine balance between victim and criminal, and the reader is torn between sympathy and horror. *Jezebel* is a fascinating psychological study that has resonance in our modern culture's celebration of youth and beauty. Dissecting the mind of a woman obsessed with beauty and haunted by the fear of growing old, Némirovsky delivers a fascinating, tragic study of how such a woman sees herself and is seen by others.

In *Jezebel*, Gladys describes her own mother, whom she detested: 'Until she was eighteen years old, she had lived with her mother, a cold woman, harsh and virtually mad, an elderly painted doll who was sometimes frivolous and sometimes terrifying . . .' In *David Golder*, *Le Bal* and *The Wine of Solitude,* Némirovsky also depicts a certain type of mother in a fiercely negative light. This was almost certainly a reflection of her antagonistic relationship with her own mother, Fanny, who dressed her daughter in children's clothing when she was well into her teens, in order to give the impression that she herself was still youthful and seductive.

At the end of World War II, the bitter relationship between mothers and daughters that Némirovsky depicted many times in fiction was to be reflected in reality. Both Némirovsky and her husband, Michel Epstein, were murdered at Auschwitz. When the war was over, Fanny Némirovsky famously refused to open her door to her granddaughters, Denise, aged fifteen and Elisabeth, aged seven, telling their guardian to take them to an orphange. Both children survived, thanks to the generosity of the publisher Albin Michel and other friends of Némirovsky.

When Fanny Némirovsky died, well into her nineties, only two things were found in the safe of her apartment: a copy of *David Golder* and a copy of *Jezebel*.

Sandra Smith
Robinson College
Cambridge

Jezebel

A woman took the stand.

She was still beautiful, despite her paleness and her drained, distraught appearance. Her sensual eyelashes were pale from crying and her mouth drooped, yet she still looked young. Her hair was hidden beneath a black hat.

Out of habit she placed her hand on her neck, no doubt feeling for the long strand of pearls she had worn in the past, but her neck was bare; she faltered; slowly, sadly, she wrung her hands and a soft whisper ran round the breathless crowd of people as they followed her every move.

'The gentlemen of the jury wish to see your face,' said the Presiding Judge. 'Remove your hat.'

She took it off and, once again, all eyes were drawn to her perfect, small, bare hands.

Her chambermaid was seated in the first row with the other witnesses. She moved instinctively as if to rise and help her mistress, then realised where she was; she blushed and looked confused.

It was a summer's day in Paris, but dull and cold; rain

1

streamed down the tall windows; a pallid orange glow lit up the old wooden panelling, the gilded coffered ceiling and the Judges' red robes. The accused woman looked at the jurors sitting opposite her, then at the courtroom, where people formed clusters in every corner.

'State your full name,' said the Judge. 'Place of birth . . . Age . . .'

It was impossible to hear what the defendant whispered.

'She said something,' murmured the women in the courtroom. 'What was it? Where was she born? . . . How old is she? . . . We can't hear a thing!'

Her hair was fine and light blonde; she was dressed in black. 'She's very good-looking,' one woman whispered, sighing with pleasure, as if she were at the theatre.

The members of the public in the standing area could not hear the reading of the charges very well. They passed the morning newspapers around to each other: every front page carried a photograph of the accused woman and an article about the crime.

The woman was called Gladys Eysenach. She had been accused of killing her lover, Bernard Martin, aged twenty.

The Judge began his interrogation: 'Where were you born?'

'Santa-Paloma.'

'That is a village between Brazil and Uruguay,' the Judge said to the jurors. 'What is your maiden name?'

'Gladys Burnera.'

'We shall not discuss your past here. I understand that your childhood and early adulthood were spent travelling in distant places, several of which have experienced political unrest and where it has been impossible to make the customary enquiries. We are therefore forced to rely, for the large part, on your own account of your early years. You have made an official statement claiming that you are the daughter of a shipowner from Montevideo, that your mother, Sophie Burnera, left your father two months after they were married, that you were born far from where he lived and that you never knew him. Is that correct?'

'Yes.'

'Your childhood was spent travelling widely. You were married when still virtually a child, as was the custom in your country; your husband was Richard Eysenach, a banker; you lost your husband in 1912. You belong to that transient circle of socialites who have no home or ties in any one particular place. You have stated that since your husband died, you have lived in South America, North America, Poland, Italy, Spain, to name but a few ... without counting the numerous cruises on your yacht that you sold in 1930. You are extremely wealthy. You inherited your fortune partly from your mother, partly from your dead husband. You lived in France on several occasions before the war and you settled here in 1928. Between 1914 and 1915 you lived near Antibes. That place and time must evoke sad memories for you: it was there that your only child, a daughter, died in 1915. After this misfortune, your life became even more unstable; you wandered from place to place. You had numerous short-lived love affairs in the period following the war, when the social climate was favourable to amorous adventures. Finally, in 1930, through mutual friends, you met Count Aldo Monti, who comes from a well-established, honourable Italian family. He asked you to marry him. The marriage was agreed, was it not?'

'Yes,' Gladys Eysenbach replied quietly.

'Your engagement was more or less official. Suddenly you decided to break it off. For what reason? You refuse to answer? Presumably you did not wish to relinquish your free, self-indulgent lifestyle and all the advantages it brought. Your fiancé became your lover. Is that correct?'

'Yes.'

'There is no sign of any other affair between 1930 and October 1934. You were faithful to Count Monti for four years. A chance encounter brought you into contact with the person who was to become your victim. He was a boy of twenty, Bernard Martin, son of a former butler and of a poor background. It is this fact that wounded your pride and was undoubtedly the reason why you denied for so long, against all the evidence, that you were having a relationship with the victim. Bernard Martin, a student at the Faculty of Literature, residing at 6 rue des Fossés-Saint-Jacques, Paris, twenty years of age, managed to seduce you, a woman of the world, who was very beautiful, rich and admired. Well? You have nothing to say? It seems that, bizarrely, scandalously, you gave in to him almost immediately; you corrupted him, gave him money and finally killed him. It is for this crime that you are on trial today.'

The defendant slowly clasped her trembling hands together; her nails dug deep into her pale skin; her colourless lips opened slightly, with difficulty, but she uttered not a word, not a sound.

'Tell the gentlemen of the jury how you met him,' the Judge said once more. 'You have nothing to say?'

'He followed me one evening,' she finally said, quietly. 'It was last autumn. I . . . I can't remember the exact date. No, I can't remember,' she repeated, sounding distraught.

'You gave the date as 12 October in your official statement.'

'Possibly,' she murmured. 'I don't remember . . .'

'Did he . . . proposition you? Come now, answer me. I understand that such an admission must be painful to you. You went home with him that very night.'

'No, no! It isn't true!' she cried softly. 'Listen to me . . .'

She said a few muffled words that no one could hear, then fell silent.

'Answer me,' said the Judge.

The accused woman turned towards the jury and the crowd of people who were watching her intently. She made a weary gesture of despair and sighed. 'I have nothing to say.'

'Well, then, you will answer my questions. You claim that you refused to speak to him that evening. Yet our enquiries have proven that the next day, 13 October, you went to see him at his home on the rue des Fossés-Saint-Jacques. Is that correct?'

'Yes,' she said. Blood rushed to her cheeks as she replied, then slowly receded, leaving her pale and trembling.

'So you were in the habit of speaking to young men who accosted you in the street? Or did you find this boy particularly attractive? You have nothing to say? You have renounced your right to secrecy about your private life.

In the High Court, in this public hearing, all the facts must be examined.'

'Yes,' she replied wearily.

'So you went to see him. What happened next? Did you see him again?'

'Yes.'

'How many times?'

'I don't remember.'

'You found him attractive? Were you in love with him?'

'No.'

'Well, then, why did you let him seduce you? Out of perversion? Out of fear? Did you fear his threats of blackmail? After his death, not a single letter from you was found at his home. Did you write to him often?'

'No.'

'Did you fear he would be indiscreet? Were you afraid that Count Monti would come to learn of your mad behaviour, your shameful affair? Was that it? Did Bernard Martin love you? Or was he pursuing you out of self-interest? You don't know? Let us move on now to the question of money. To avoid tarnishing the memory of your victim, you did not reveal a fact that came to light by chance during our enquiries. How much money did you give to Bernard Martin during your brief affair that lasted from 13 October 1934 to 24 December of the same year? The unfortunate young man was murdered on the night of Christmas Eve 1934. How much money did he receive from you during those two months?'

'I didn't give him any money.'

'Yes you did. We found a cheque dated 15 November 1934 for the sum of five thousand francs made payable to him and signed by you. The money was deposited the following day. No one knows what it was used for. Did you give him any more money?'

'No.'

'Another cheque for five thousand francs was also found. It seems to be a fixed amount but it was never cashed.'

'That's right,' murmured the defendant.

'Let us move on to the crime itself, shall we? I assume it's not as difficult to talk about it as it was to do it. On that night, Christmas Eve of last year, you left your house at eight-thirty in the evening with Count Monti. You dined with him at a restaurant, Chez Ciro. You were to meet your mutual friends, the Perciers, Henri Percier, a Minister in the current government, and his wife. All four of you went to a nightclub where you danced until three o'clock in the morning. Is that correct?'

'Yes.'

'Count Monti took you home and said goodbye to you at your door. In your statement, you claimed that when the car stopped in front of your house, you spotted Bernard Martin hiding in the doorway. That is correct, is it not? Had you agreed to meet him that night?'

'No. I hadn't seen him for some time.'

'Exactly how long had it been?'

'About ten days.'

'Why? You had decided to break it off? You refuse to answer? When you saw him in the street that December morning, what did he say to you?'

'He wanted to come inside.'

'And then?'

'I refused. He was drunk, that much was obvious. I

was afraid. When I opened the door, I realised he'd followed me in. He came into my bedroom.'

'What did he say to you?'

'He threatened to tell everything to Aldo Monti, whom I loved.'

'You had a strange way of showing him your love!'

'I loved him,' she insisted.

'And then?'

'I was frightened. I begged him. He laughed at me. He pushed me aside. At that very moment, the telephone rang. Only Aldo Monti would be calling me at that hour. Bernard Martin grabbed the telephone. He wanted to answer it. I . . . I took the gun from the drawer of my bedside table. I fired . . . I didn't know what I was doing any more.'

'Really? That's what murderers always say.'

'It's still the truth,' Gladys Eysenach said quietly.

'Let us assume so. When you realised what had happened, what did you do?'

'He was lying there in front of me, dead. I wanted to try to resuscitate him, but I could see it was too late.'

'And then?'

'Then . . . My chambermaid called the police. That's everything.'

'Really? And when the police arrived and the crime was discovered, you openly admitted what you had done?'

'No.'

'What did you say?'

'I said that I had just got home,' replied Gladys Eysenach in a choked voice, 'and that while I was undressing in the adjoining bathroom, I heard a noise and opened the door to find an intruder.'

'Who was about to steal your jewellery, the jewellery you'd taken off and left on the dressing table, isn't that so?'

'Yes, that's correct.'

'The lie was quite believable,' said the Judge, turning towards the jury, 'for the great wealth and social position of the accused easily placed her beyond suspicion. Unfortunately for her, when the detectives arrived, the defendant was still wearing her ermine coat, evening gown and all her jewellery. The next day the examining magistrate interrogated her in the most skilful way. I would not hesitate in deeming her deposition a model of its type. It is excellent. It is cruel, I do not deny this, but excellent. This woman hesitates, ties herself up in knots, as the common saying goes, becomes confused, lies, withdraws her statements. She swears, and so very sincerely, that Bernard Martin was never her lover, insisting upon this fact in spite of all the plausible, logical evidence. She cries, she begs and, finally, she confesses. The examining magistrate skilfully and concisely analyses the situation, questions her intensely and succeeds in reconstructing the events, which prove, alas, quite commonplace. An ageing woman, attracted by the youth of this boy, enticed by a stranger, by the excitement of a sexual encounter, perhaps even by the humble situation of her lover – who can say? This woman, a woman who was clearly bored by her affairs with men of her own social status, yields to him, then wishes to break it off, believing, with the arrogance of a wealthy woman, that her lover has been paid off, that he will be content with her charity, that he will disappear out of her life. But this young boy – who has never known any women apart from prostitutes and girls he's met at cafés – cannot forget her beauty, her prestige. He pursues her, threatens her. She becomes frightened and kills him. This deposition is truly moving. At every question the magistrates asks, she first tries to defend herself, then confesses, replying "yes, yes" . . . This word constantly recurs. She explains nothing. She is ashamed. She is wasting away out of shame, as you can see, gentlemen of the jury! But the analysis of her crime, the chain of events proposed to her is so believable, so crystal clear, so logical that she cannot defend herself. "Yes", she keeps saying and "Yes" to the most serious question: "Was the murder premeditated?" She then retracts her statement, realising the importance of her response. She claims she committed the murder in a moment of madness. Why, then, I ask the defendant, why did you live your entire life without owning a weapon and yet within three weeks of meeting Bernard Martin you bought a gun, a gun which you kept with you at all times?'

'No, it was kept in a drawer in my bedside table.'

'Why did you buy it?'

'I don't know . . .'

'That's rather an odd reply. Come, now, tell the truth! Did you plan to kill Bernard Martin?'

'No,' she replied, her voice shaking, 'I swear it.'

'Whom did you intend to use it on then? Yourself? Count Monti, who was apparently making you feel jealous? A rival?'

'No, no,' the accused woman replied, hiding her face in her hands. 'No more questions! I won't say anything else. I've confessed to everything, everything you wanted me to!'

'Very well, then. We shall proceed to the testimony of the witnesses. Usher, bring in the first witness.'

A woman walked in; tears were streaming down her sallow face; her glistening eyes looked with terror from the stand to the Judges in their scarlet robes. Outside, the rain kept falling with its steady pattering. One of the journalists was getting bored; he jotted down sentences on the sheet of paper in front of him that could have come straight out of a novel: 'The wind drew deep sighs from the golden plane trees that lined the Seine.'

'State your full name.'

'Flora Adèle Larivière.'

'State your age.'

'Thirty-two.'

'Your profession?'

'Personal chambermaid to Madame Eysenach.'

'You are not being sworn in, so I am invoking my discretionary powers to question you. When did you first enter the service of the accused?'

'It will be seven years on the 19 January.'

'Tell us what you know of the crime. Your mistress was to celebrate Christmas Eve in the company of Count Monti, was she not?'

'Yes, Your Honour.'

'Did she tell you what time she would be coming home?'

'She said it would be quite late. She told me I wasn't to wait up for her.'

'Was that usual? Or did you normally wait up for her?'

'I had been very ill a month earlier and I was still very

tired. Madame wasn't like most mistresses; she looked after her employees. She spoke to me with great kindness: "You wear yourself out too much, my poor Flora. I absolutely forbid you to wait up for me. I'll get undressed by myself."'

'Did she appear quite normal that evening? Was she nervous, agitated?'

'No, just sad. She was often sad. I'd seen her crying more than once.'

'Do you know why she was crying?'

'The Count was making her jealous.'

'Return to what happened that evening.'

'Madame went out and I went to bed; my bedroom is upstairs, separated from Madame's room by a hallway. I was awakened by the sound of the telephone ringing. I remember that I could just about see light coming through the curtains. It must have been four or five o'clock in the morning. Sometimes Count Monti would call her after she'd come home. Madame probably wanted to be sure he had gone straight home after leaving her. Actually, she would sometimes call him straight back, pretending she wanted to hear his voice one more time. So I heard the phone ringing but no one was answering. That worried me; I could sense something was wrong. I got up and went into the hallway and listened. I heard Madame and a man's voice and almost immediately afterwards a gunshot.'

'And then?'

'I was absolutely terrified. I rushed to the bedroom, but then, I don't know why, I didn't dare go in. I listened at the door. I couldn't hear a single sound, not even a whisper, nothing. I opened the door and went in. I'll never forget it. Madame was sitting on the bed, still fully dressed, in her ermine coat, her evening gown and jewellery. Her face was lit up by a small lamp on her dressing table. She wasn't crying. She looked pale and frightened. I called out to her, grabbed hold of her arm. "Madame, Madame!" I cried. She seemed not to hear anything. Finally, she looked at me and said, "Flora, I've killed him." The first thing I thought of was that she had killed her lover . . . that she had quarrelled with the Count and shot him in a moment of madness. I looked around. I was so shaken up and the bedroom was so dimly lit that at first all I saw was a dark shape lying on the ground, as if someone had thrown a pile of clothes on the floor. I switched on the light and saw that the telephone had been knocked to the ground and next to it was the gun. Then I saw there was a man stretched out on the floor. Mother Mary, I leaned down and couldn't believe my eyes. It wasn't Count Monti. It was some young man I'd never seen before.'

'You had never seen the victim before? Not at your mistress's house or anywhere else?'

'Never, Your Honour.'

'The defendant had never mentioned his name in front of you?'

'Never, Your Honour; I'd never heard his name.'

'When you saw the body of the unfortunate young man, what did you do?'

'I thought that he might still be breathing and said so to Madame. She stood up and then knelt down beside me. She raised the head of the . . . of Bernard Martin . . . she lifted his head and held it like that for a few moments.

13

She looked at him without saying a word, without moving, and it was true, there was nothing we could do. Blood was dripping out of the corner of his mouth. He looked very young and undernourished; he was thin, with hollow cheeks, and his clothes were wet, as if he'd been outdoors for a long time. It was raining that night. I said, "There's nothing we can do. He's dead." Madame didn't reply. She couldn't take her eyes off him. She reached for her evening bag, but kept staring at Bernard Martin. She took a handkerchief out of her bag. She wiped away the blood and froth that was running out of the corner of his mouth. She sighed deeply, then looked at me as if she were coming back to her senses. Then she stood up and said to me, "Call the police, my dear Flora." When she said "dear" . . . it . . . I can't explain how that felt to me. It was almost as if Madame realised she would be all alone from that moment on and that she considered me almost a friend. I was the one who said, "He was a burglar, wasn't he?"'

'And that was what you truly believed, was it?'

'No, it wasn't. I have to tell the truth, don't I? But I couldn't believe that Madame, who was so sweet, so kind to everyone, could have killed someone like that without good reason. I thought he was a blackmailer who had threatened her.'

'Your loyalty to your mistress is commendable. Nevertheless, it should not have led you to advise the defendant to tell a childish lie that could only make her situation worse. What did the accused reply?'

'She didn't. She left the room. She walked into the hallway. She was wringing her hands, like she's doing now. Then she went to my room and threw herself down on my bed. She didn't budge from there until the police arrived. It was cold. I wanted to cover her legs with a blanket. I noticed she was asleep. She only woke up when the policemen came in. That's all I know.'

'Do the members of the jury or the Prosecuting Attorney wish to ask this witness any questions?'

'Mademoiselle Larivière,' said the Prosecuting Attorney, 'you have demonstrated a most commendable loyalty and done your utmost to portray the accused as a sweet, kind woman loved by her servants. I do not dispute this. But you have very adeptly avoided any mention of her morals. We shall not discuss her documented affairs, in particular her relationship with a young Englishman, George Canning, killed in action in 1916, or Herbert Lacy, whom the accused met in 1925 when she returned to Paris after a long absence. Nor shall we delve into all her other former affairs. But you have been employed by the defendant since 1928. Have you known her to have any lovers during that time?'

'Count Monti.'

'That is a matter of public knowledge. And apart from Count Monti?'

'There's been no one since she met the Count; I would swear to it.'

'Of course you would.'

'I don't understand . . .'

'Let us move on. Before Count Monti, can you be certain that your mistress had no one else in her life?'

'She never confided in me.'

'I understand. But did you not tell one of your friends that Madame, and I am quoting you word for word here, "must have had very deep feelings for the Count to have stopped chasing men". Did you say that?'

'Yes, but what I meant . . .'

'Did you say that: yes or no?'

'Yes. Madame had lovers before the Count, but she was a free woman, a widow with no children.'

'Perhaps. Nevertheless, the defence should not portray the accused as a woman beyond reproach, who had fallen under the spell of a scoundrel. I intend to show, and the gentlemen of the jury will come to see, that Gladys Eysenach was no innocent, and that it would be extraordinary to believe that this young man, Bernard Martin, was capable of frightening her to the point of forcing her to commit murder. The defendant claims she is the victim here. But how do we know that Bernard Martin was not the true victim of this woman? There is an attempt to discredit Bernard Martin, gentlemen of the jury; he is being portrayed as some sort of gigolo, some low-life pimp, while in fact he was a well-behaved, studious young man. No one has the right to cast such vile aspersions on his character! The victim, who was studying for his Bachelor's Degree, lived in the poorest way in the Latin Quarter, in one small room in a third-rate hostel. After his death, all that was found was the sum of four hundred francs. Inexpensive clothing, no jewellery. Is that, I ask you, the lifestyle of a gigolo, adored by a rich woman whom he obsessively and constantly threatened? How do you know that it was not this woman, a woman empowered by her beauty, her wealth and her social standing, this woman, gentlemen of the jury, whom you see before you, who did not ensnare this young boy in order to corrupt him and then murder him? A high-society courtesan can be even more formidable than others because she is more beautiful, more worldly wise. But let us expose the hypocrisy of glorifying such women while we pour scorn on more common ladies of the night. The Gladys Eysenachs of this world must own their lovers' souls, and their lives. The accused has deceived Count Monti. She clearly played on the feelings of this noble gentleman, since she had no qualms about betraying him with a complete stranger. She found it amusing to drive Bernard Martin mad. But the game was becoming dangerous. She bought a gun and then, coldly, mercilessly, killed a young man who, had it not been for her, would have been able to continue his studies and grow into a happy adult, a man who might have become – who can say? – a valuable member of society.'

'Mademoiselle Larivière,' said the Attorney for the Defence, 'let me ask you something, if you please. Did your mistress love Count Monti? Please reply using your woman's instincts.'

'She adored him.'

'Thank you. This single word is all the reply needed to respond to the Prosecuting Attorney's moving eloquence. It is a humble word, but so honest: *adored*. She adored her lover. She was in love, jealous, and so perhaps in a moment of folly might she not have wished to arouse her fickle lover's jealousy? Might she not have given in to this young man who was pursuing her? Might she not have regretted it afterwards, feared the scandal, leading her to kill in a moment of madness, a moment she will pay for, and for the rest of her life? Does this not seem simpler, more humane, more logical than attempting to transform this woman – who is, of course, guilty of this crime, I do not deny it, but who is charming and kind – into some sort of fiend or femme fatale from the cinema?'

The Judge excused the witness. The accused woman seemed overcome by fatigue. Her face, when revealing any emotion at all, showed only a troubled weariness. Her chambermaid smiled shyly at her as she left the courtroom, as if to give her courage, and the defendant began to cry. Tears streamed down her pale cheeks. She wiped them away with the back of her hand, then lowered her eyes and sat totally still.

Outside, it was still raining. The sky was growing darker. The lights were switched on. Beneath the yellowish glare, the accused woman's face looked suddenly tragic, ageless; it was motionless; her soul seemed to have sought refuge within her deep-set, beautiful, haunted eyes.

'Usher,' said the Judge, 'bring in the next witness.'

It was stiflingly hot; the young attorneys sitting on the floor, some in the courtroom itself, formed a black carpet.

'Please state your full name,' said the Judge.

'Aldo de Fieschi, Count Monti.'

He was a man in his forties, very tall, clean-shaven, with a handsome face and regular features, a harsh mouth, light-grey eyes and long eyelashes.

A member of the public leaned towards a woman and whispered in her ear, 'Poor Aldo. Do you know what he said to me the day after the crime? He was crushed, and he'd lost all his coolness and composure. "Ah!, why didn't she kill me instead?" he said. He'll never forgive her for causing such shame, such a display of depravity . . .'

'How do you know? Men are so strange. She undoubtedly slept with that young Bernard Martin to make him jealous. She killed him so that Monti wouldn't find out. He should be flattered . . .'

'That's the defence's argument.'

Meanwhile, the Judge was asking the witness: 'Did you spend the evening of the crime with the defendant?'

'Yes, Your Honour.'

'You met the accused in 1930?'

'That is correct.'

'You wished to marry her?'

'Yes, Your Honour.'

'Gladys Eysenach agreed to marry you at first. Then she changed her mind, did she not?'

'Yes, she changed her mind.'

'What were her reasons?'

'Madame Eysenach was reluctant to give up her freedom.'

'And she gave no other reasons?'

'No, she did not.'

'Did you ask her again?'

'Yes, several times.'

'And each time she refused?'

'That is correct.'

'Did you have the feeling that, more recently, the accused had a secret lover in her life? Did you fear you might have a rival?'

'No, I did not.'

'Tell us about the evening before the crime, the last evening that you and the accused spent together.'

'I had gone to collect Madame Eysenach at her house,

19

at about eight-thirty. She seemed quite normal, not nervous or sad. We had dinner at Ciro's. We spent the rest of the evening at Chez Florence with our mutual friends, the Perciers, and left at about three o'clock in the morning. My car was being repaired that day, so we used Madame Eysenach's. I took her to her door, then I went home.'

'Did you see her go inside?'

'I was about to get out of the car, naturally, to see her in, but I hadn't been feeling well all day. I'd kept myself going with aspirin. I started shivering in the car. Madame Eysenach was worried and immediately begged me not to get out. It was freezing that night. I remember it was raining and extremely windy. Nevertheless, I only laughed when she said she was worried about me. The war taught me how to put up with such problems, and many others, without attaching any importance to them. We even had a little fight about it, but jokingly. I wanted to open the door and get out, but Madame Eysenach wouldn't let me. She pushed my hand away and jumped out on to the pavement. "Take the Count back home," she called out to the driver. I had just enough time to kiss her hand before the car pulled away.'

'Presumably she had spotted Bernard Martin who was waiting for her?'

'Presumably,' Count Monti replied curtly.

'And you had no contact with Madame Eysenach until the next day?'

'When I got home, I telephoned her, as we had arranged. No one answered. I thought that Madame Eysenach was already asleep. It was a little after six o'clock when I was awakened by Flora, her chambermaid, who told me the terrible news. She asked me to come at once, not to delay a second, that something dreadful had happened. You can imagine how frightened I was. I quickly got dressed and rushed out of the house. By the time I got to Madame Eysenach's, the police had been called. I found the house full of people and the body of the unfortunate young man was already cold.'

'Had you ever seen the victim before?'

'Never.'

'And you had never heard his name spoken, naturally.'

'Not once.'

'Gentlemen of the jury, do you have any questions to ask this witness? The Prosecuting Attorney? The Attorney for the Defence?'

'Monsieur,' asked the Attorney for the Defence, 'would you please tell the court if it is true that the accused displayed jealousy over your attentions to one of her friends, as has been said? Did she ever make those kinds of remarks to you?'

'I don't remember,' replied Count Monti.

'Try to think back, would you?'

'Actually,' the witness finally said, 'Madame Eysenach has been jealous and irritable; recently, that is . . .'

'Yes,' said the Attorney for the Defence, barely concealing his triumph, 'since before the time when she first met Bernard Martin? Would that not be consistent with what I have just been attempting to demonstrate to the jury: this lonely, misunderstood woman, seeking some meagre consolation, some crumbs of love from a stranger after being deceived and scorned by the man she adored?'

'I never stopped caring for her,' said the Count, his

large, delicate hands nervously gripping the edge of the witness box.

'Never? Really?'

'I had the utmost affection for Madame Eysenach; my greatest desire was to marry her, to make a home with her. She did not want the same thing. It cannot be held against me if I occasionally indulged in completely innocent attentions for which the defence seems to wish to reproach me!'

'Quite so,' said the Judge, turning towards the accused. 'It was up to you to lead an honourable life, but you clearly preferred the thrill of danger and adventure in your love life, didn't you?'

She didn't reply. Everyone could see she was shaking.

The Attorney for the Defence continued questioning Count Monti: 'Is it possible, Sir, that you – you, whom this unfortunate woman loved – might substantiate the claim that a poor woman, weak and in love, might be turned into a depraved, mad creature? Who more than you should show her compassion? If she had felt that you were sincere in your affection, might that not have saved her? Ah,' he said, ever so slightly raising his famous voice with its golden tones, 'ah, you are forcing me to go into embarrassing detail, sir. I detest doing so, but nevertheless . . . I do ask you to forgive me, sir, but I am going to have to be brutally honest. Regarding your financial situation, Count Monti: were you not going through a difficult time when you first met Madame Eysenach?'

In the press section, the journalists were taking notes: 'Disturbance in the court. The Judge calls for an adjournment. When court resumes, the witness states . . .'

'The truth is that my family, which is wealthier in property than in money, has never had an income to match its social standing. Nevertheless, I do not believe you could find anyone in either Italy or Paris who could honestly accuse me of having run up debts or lived in an extravagant manner. To me, Madame Eysenach's considerable wealth was less important than her attractiveness and personal qualities. I did not consider her wealth as an obstacle to our marriage since, once married, I hoped to set myself up in a suitable and highly successful business. I was offering my fiancée a family name that would allow her to forget my relative lack of money. It is strange that I am being reproached for this financial embarrassment which, sadly, in a noble Roman family, is normally of no surprise to anyone ...'

'The court defers', said the Judge, 'to the witness's excellent explanation. You may step down, sir. Usher, bring in the next witness.'

A very beautiful woman entered the witness box, wearing a luxurious fox coat. She was slim with pale skin and angular features; a short black veil fell over her eyes. She slowly took off her long black gloves in order to be sworn in.

'State your full name.'

'Jeannine Marie Suzanne Percier.'

'State your age.'

'Twenty-five.'

'Address.'

'8 rue de la Faisanderie.'

'Profession.'

'None.'

'You have been summoned as a witness, Madame, as the fourth member of the party at dinner on the evening of the crime and also as a close friend of the accused. Is that correct?'

'Gladys Eysenach was a very close friend of mine, that is true. I was terribly fond of her. I still feel deep sympathy for her and, naturally, immense pity . . .'

She turned to look at the defendant and smiled at her, as if prompting her to smile back, to show some gratitude for her kindness. Gladys Eysenach raised her head with difficulty and stared at the witness; her mouth tightened slightly with bitterness. For a moment the two women locked eyes, then the accused woman shivered and wrapped the collar of her coat round her tighter and hid her face.

'Were you privy to the details of your friend's love life?'

'Good Lord, Your Honour, you must know what female friendship is like? Of course we talk a lot . . . We recommend dressmakers to each other, we go out together, but it is rare that we confide in each other. I knew about the relationship between Gladys and Count Monti as everyone did. But whether there was anyone apart from Count Monti I couldn't say, at least, not for sure . . .'

'Do you know why your friend continued stubbornly to refuse Count Monti's offer of marriage?'

'I imagine', said Jeannine Percier, shrugging her shoulders slightly, 'that she was determined to keep her freedom; it was something she valued highly, judging from the way she used it.'

'Can you be more precise, Madame?'

'I don't want to say anything bad – Heaven forbid – I'm only telling you what everyone knew. Gladys was excessively flirtatious. She enjoyed nothing more than compliments, adoration, but that's not a crime.'

'Quite so, just so long as it stops there.'

'My husband and I had the greatest friendship for Count Monti and we often warned him about a marriage which, in my humble opinion, might have made both of them unhappy.'

'And yet their relationship was a happy one?'

'It seemed to be. But poor Gladys was painfully and excessively jealous. She was also highly emotional underneath a very sweet exterior. When I heard about the horrible crime, I was not surprised. It always seemed to me that there was something deeply tragic within Gladys. She was ... mysterious ... She was unreasonably demanding. She required men to be faithful to her in a way that is no longer customary, unfortunately! She expected a kind of devotion that was justified by her beauty, of course, but as for her age ... She refused to accept these things. She couldn't admit that her lover's passion had cooled, that he was still extremely fond of her, of course, but that it was perhaps time for her to be more indulgent, more tolerant ... And since her own emotions were very intense, all these things influenced her personality and made her moody and irritable.'

'Can you tell us about the night before the crime, the Christmas Eve dinner that was to end so tragically?'

'My husband and I met Gladys and the Count at Ciro's, where we all had dinner. We decided to go on to Chez

Florence to round off the evening. The rest of the night was uneventful. We drank champagne, danced and left in the early hours of the morning. That's all.'

'Did the accused seem nervous, anxious?'

'She seemed excessively nervous and anxious that night, Your Honour. Every time Count Monti looked at another woman, oh, sometimes perfectly innocently, every time he made some banal compliment to the woman sitting next to him, the poor thing turned white and started trembling. It was pitiful, I can tell you. I would have liked to reassure her, but how could I? I remember I gave her a big hug, from the bottom of my heart when we said goodbye, and I hoped she could feel my sympathy. I'm happy that I gave in to that spontaneous show of affection, now that I can imagine what the poor woman has had to endure since then.'

'Did you ever see Bernard Martin at the defendant's home?'

'Never, Your Honour.'

'Did you ever hear his name spoken?'

'Never.'

'Have you knowledge of any other similar relationships, either directly from the accused woman herself or from a third party? I see you are hesitating. Do not forget that you are under oath.'

'Really,' said Jeannine Percier, nervously twisting her long gloves, 'I don't know what to say . . .'

'Just tell the truth, Madame, that's all. Would you prefer me to ask you questions? You stated that you were not surprised at the crime, that something was bound to happen, that Madame Eysenach was fated, sooner or later, to fall prey to some scoundrel or other. I am quoting your very own words.'

'If that's what I said in my statement, it's because it is true.'

'Would you please be more precise, Madame? You are here to enlighten the court.'

'When I said that, I have to admit I was thinking about a . . . a house on the rue Balzac that the unfortunate woman had a weakness to visit often.'

'Are you saying it was a bordello?'

'Yes. I don't think it's right to hide from the court those meetings which, however strange and abnormal they are, might shed some light on the pathological side of the personality of my poor dear friend.'

The Judge looked at Gladys Eysenach. 'Is this true?'

'Yes,' she replied wearily.

The Judge slowly raised his arms in their large, scarlet sleeves. 'What sort of shameful pleasure were you seeking in such a place? You are still beautiful, in a relationship with a nobleman: whatever possessed you to sleep with strangers? You are even rich, so do not have the excuse that you needed the money, a situation that, sadly, is the undoing of many women. You have nothing to say?'

'I can't say it's not true,' the accused woman said softly.

'Has the witness finished her testimony?'

'Yes, Your Honour. May I be allowed to beg the jury for clemency on behalf of this unfortunate woman?'

'That is the role of the defence, not yours,' said the Judge, smiling almost imperceptibly. 'You may step down, Madame.'

She left the witness box and other witnesses came and went. They were not very important people: the concierge of the building where the accused lived, her chauffeur. They gave their testimony in an awkward, comical way, but all of them were clearly trying to do everything in their power to paint a good picture of Gladys Eysenach. Then came the doctors, some spoke of the accused woman's mental state, 'nervous, excitable, but sound of mind and responsible for her actions'; others described the body of the victim.

The crowd was tired and there was a constant subdued hum of noise: certain words, certain gestures that the witnesses made, a word, a twitch, an inflexion of the voice, caused the courtroom to resound with low, anxious laughter.

'Bring in the next witness.'

He was an elderly man with pale, almost transparent skin and white hair; at the corners of his long, delicate mouth were the fine lines of weariness that betray physical decline. When she saw him, the accused woman let out a sad little sigh; then she leaned forward to look at him more closely.

She was crying now; she looked old and tired, thoroughly ashamed, defeated . . .

'State your full name.'

'Claude-Patrice Beauchamp.'

'Your age?'

'Seventy-one.'

'Address?'

'28 boulevard du Mail, Vevey, Switzerland.'

'Profession?'

'No profession.'

'You must speak louder so that the gentlemen of the jury can hear you. Are you able to do that?'

The witness nodded, then said softly, forcing himself to speak as clearly as possible, 'Yes, Your Honour. Please forgive me. I am old and not well.'

'Would you like to sit down?'

He refused.

'You are a close relative of the defendant, her only living relative, in fact, are you not?'

'Gladys Eysenach's maiden name was Burnera. I was married to Teresa Burnera. My wife's father and Gladys Eysenach's father were brothers, wealthy shipowners from Montevideo. Salvador Burnera, my cousin's father, was an exceedingly intelligent and sophisticated man. Unfortunately, he and his wife were separated and my cousin was raised by her mother who was, in my opinion, a person with a rather difficult, unstable character. She had broken off all contact with her close relatives. My wife met her cousin for the first time during a visit to Aix-les-Bains; Gladys Eysenach was still almost a child at the time . . . My wife invited her to come and spend the summer with us in London, where we lived then.'

'How long ago was that?'

The witness did not reply. He looked at the accused woman with pity; her face seemed haggard and drained beneath the bright lights. She sadly lowered her eyes.

'It was a long time ago,' he said, sighing. 'I can't remember . . .'

'Can you tell the gentlemen of the jury about the accused woman's character at that time?'

'She was sweet and happy then. Eager for compliments. She liked being courted more than anything.'

'Did you continue to see her?'

'Occasionally. She had married Richard Eysenach. She travelled constantly. Whenever she was in Paris, I always made a point of going to see her to pay my respects. But I was rarely in Paris. My wife's health was delicate and we lived in Switzerland for several months of the year. But my son, Olivier, was often a guest at the Eysenachs' house. In 1914, a few months before the death of poor little Marie-Thérèse (my cousin's daughter), I was passing through Antibes. We saw each other there. Then I went back to Vevey. My son was killed in the war. I settled in Vevey for good because the climate suited me. I didn't see my cousin again.'

'You are seeing her today for the first time in twenty years?'

'Yes, Your Honour.'

'You have been called as a witness in this painful case because a letter addressed to you was found in the defendant's home. We have that letter here. It will be read to the gentlemen of the jury.'

The accused woman lowered her head and heard her letter read out:

Please come and help me . . . Don't be surprised that I am appealing to you . . . I imagine you've forgotten all about me? . . . But I have no one else in the world. Everyone else is dead. I am so alone. Sometimes I feel as if I have been buried alive, in a pit of loneliness. You alone can remember the woman I used to be. I am ashamed, desperately ashamed, but I want to have the courage to ask your help, you and only you, because you once loved me . . .

'This letter was stamped and addressed to you in Switzerland, but it was never posted.'

'And I deeply regret that,' Beauchamp said quietly.

'I wish the defendant to tell me if she wrote this with the intention of confiding in her relative.'

She stood up with difficulty and nodded. 'Yes . . .'

'Did you wish to tell him about Bernard Martin? Share your concerns with him over this relationship? Ask his advice? It is regrettable that you did not follow through with your initial plan . . .'

'Perhaps,' she replied, slowly shrugging her shoulders.

'Will the witness please tell us whether the accused wrote him any letters in recent months?'

'Never. The last letter I received from her was the one she wrote telling me of her daughter's death.'

'In your opinion, was the defendant capable of an act of violence?'

'No, Your Honour.'

'Very well. Thank you.'

He left. Other witnesses were shown into the box. Gladys looked up now and again, as if she were trying to find the face of a friend in the crowd. The very people whose curiosity had been so painful to her a few hours earlier now looked away; they were already weary, morose, indifferent. The crowd was beginning to feel the excitement and tiredness that comes at the end of a trial. Through a

31

badly closed door, waves of noise from the corridor occasionally reached the courtroom, like the sea washing against a little island. The members of the public coldly examined the trembling, pale, haggard face of the accused, like people looking at a wild animal, imprisoned behind the bars of its cage: savage but confined, its teeth and nails pulled out, panting, half dead ...

There were sniggers, shrugs of the shoulder, muffled exclamations. Everyone was whispering: 'How disappointing ... People said she was so beautiful but she looks like an old woman ...'

'Come on, be fair. I'd like to see what you'd look like after being held in custody for months, wearing no make-up at all, not to mention the remorse she must be feeling ...'

'Thanks very much!'

'She's attractive; that's undeniable ... She's slim ... Look at how beautiful her hands are ... Hands that committed murder ...'

'Still, it isn't very common for rich people to commit murder.'

'She's proof ...'

In the very back row of the standing gallery a woman sighed. 'Imagine cheating on a lover like Count Monti ...'

The witnesses now being heard were people who had known Bernard Martin, but the indifferent crowd was barely listening any more. In this trial, only the accused woman was exciting; the victim was no more than a vague ghost. The apathetic public learned that Bernard Martin was born in Beix (Alpes-Maritimes) on 13 April 1915, and that the names of his mother and father were not known. Later in his life he had been legally acknowledged as the son of Martial Martin, a butler, who cohabited with Berthe Souprosse, a cook. Both had been in the service of the Dukes de Joux, who had provided them with an income until they died, Martial Martin in 1919 and Berthe Souprosse in 1932. Berthe seemed genuinely to have loved little Bernard. She had raised him attentively and in a manner that was quite above her station. The boy had been awarded a scholarship to the Lycée Louis-le-Grand.

A statement from one of Bernard Martin's former teachers was read out to the court: '"A gloomy, bitter, silent character. Exceptionally intelligent, with some indication of a genius in the making, or at least the kind of tenacity and deep, insightful patience which, when focused on a specific topic, appears as genius."

'This is an extract from my personal notes that date from the time when the poor child was reaching adolescence. I can add, now that I have searched my memory, that these gifts of patience and foresight were most often employed in the quest for vain amusement. Bernard Martin's only passion seemed to be to solve some current problem, whatever it might have been, and once he had done so, he immediately lost interest in the work or the game he had managed to master. When he was a young boy, he learned English in three months, all by himself, using only a dictionary, as the result of a bet with one of his classmates. Having reached a certain level of competence in the language, he suddenly stopped studying it and never again said a single word in English. A born mathematician, one of the best in my class, he was accepted at university, as I had predicted, doubtlessly still motivated by the same perverse curiosity and keen ambition that I found he had at the age of twelve. It was very difficult to influence him. He was the kind of boy who could not be improved by mixing with the right people, or corrupted by a bad crowd. He seemed to live according to his own laws and to obey only his own code of conduct.

'He had modest tastes, even displaying a certain leaning towards asceticism, and he was extremely ambitious; the role of the affectionate lover of a wealthy woman seems totally out of character for him. He must surely have been seduced by the status of a woman in high society: he suffered because of the obscure nature of his birth and wished to make his way in the world.

'I deplore the tragedy that cost him his life, for I always believed the boy to have a promising future.'

'Bring in the next witness.'

It was a young lad of about twenty who looked as if he came from the east Mediterranean. His black hair was badly cut and he had a dry face that seemed very emotional. He spoke quickly, mumbling a bit, embarrassed no doubt by his foreign accent.

'State your name.'

'Constantin Slotis.'

'Age?'

'Twenty.'

'Your address?'

'6 rue des Fossés-Saint-Jacques.'

'Profession?'

'Medical student.'

'You are neither related to nor a friend of the accused. You do not work for her nor does she work for you. Do you swear to speak without prejudice and with no fear of telling the truth, the whole truth and nothing but the truth? Raise your hand and say, "I so do swear." Did you know Bernard Martin?'

'We were neighbours.'

'Did he ever confide in you?'

'Never. He wasn't the type. He never talked much.'

'What type of man was he, in your opinion?'

'Sarcastic, violent, not very sociable. We had some friends in common, men and women. Everyone will tell you the same thing.'

'Did he have financial problems?'

'We all did. What I mean, Your Honour, is that in the Latin Quarter we live fairly well from the first day of the month to the fifth, but that's about it.'

'Did he ever borrow money from you?'

'No, but he would have had a hard time doing it. You don't go looking for water in a dry river, as the saying goes where I come from.'

'Did you have the impression that his financial resources had increased shortly before his death?'

'No, Your Honour.'

'Did you ever meet the defendant when she visited Bernard Martin at his home?'

'I only saw her once, on 13 October 1934.'

'Your recollection seems very precise!'

'I had an exam the next day and the perfume the woman wore was so strong that I could smell it through my door. It prevented me from working. The next day I got a very bad mark. That's why I remember the circumstances so well.'

The people in the courtroom started laughing.

'When she left,' Slotis continued, 'well, I opened my door to get a look at her. She was very beautiful. That's her all right.'

'Did she remain at your friend's very long?'

'Half an hour.'

'Did you ever speak to Bernard Martin about her visit?'

'Yes. I ran into him that same evening at a bordello on the rue Vavin. We were a little drunk, I think . . . I said to him, "Well, my pal, you're doing all right for yourself," you know, the kind of thing you say when something like that happens. He laughed. He had a very harsh look on his face as he laughed. I even thought: "Now there's a woman who's going to get it . . . one day . . ."'

'He was the one who "got it", as you put it. What did he say then?'

'He recited Athalie's dream to me, Your Honour.'

'What?'

'*My mother Jezebel appeared before me . . .*'

'That is quite a chastisement,' said the Judge, looking at Gladys Eysenach.

She was listening to Slotis with intense attention; her delicate nostrils were flaring; her bright eyes stared; a sly, cruel expression appeared on her beautiful, ravaged face, an expression that was the stock image of a murderer. The members of the public watching felt even more confident that they had the right to judge her.

'Did the witness see Bernard Martin on the eve of his death?'

'Yes. He was completely drunk.'

'Did he normally drink?'

'Rarely, and he could usually hold his liquor, but that night he was completely depressed. He was very upset about the death of one of his former mistresses, Laurette, Laure Pellegrain, who had lived with him until last November. She had tuberculosis. She died in Switzerland.'

'Did you know about this woman?' the Judge asked Gladys.

'Yes,' she replied with difficulty.

'And the money that you gave to your young lover went to this woman, did it not?'

'It's possible.'

'Look at her,' a man in the courtroom whispered in his neighbour's ear, 'look at the defendant. She must have suffered a lot because of that Bernard Martin. Sometimes when they talk about him, a look of hatred spreads across her face. But apart from that, she doesn't look like a woman who has killed someone.'

A young blonde with milky white skin and wisps of hair peeking out from under her black hat stepped into the witness box, folding her large red hands in front of her. Her name, Eugenie Wildchild, made the public laugh; even she seemed amused when she heard it.

The Judge banged the table with the paperknife he was holding. 'It is not appropriate to laugh,' he said. 'This is not some sort of show.'

'I'm only laughing because I'm nervous.'

'Well, compose yourself and answer the questions. You are employed by Madame Dumont, owner of the building on the rue des Fossés-Saint-Jacques where the victim resided. Do you recognise the defendant as the person who visited Bernard Martin on several occasions?'

'Yes, Your Honour,' the girl replied, 'I recognise her.'

'Did you see her often?'

'Do you think that, in student lodgings, you remember all the women who come? But her, I noticed her particularly, because she wasn't like the others; she had beautiful clothes and wore a fox stole. But I don't remember whether she came three, four or five times. It was something like that . . .'

'Did Bernard Martin ever confide in you?'

'Him? Really!'

'He doesn't seem to have left you with a very nice impression.'

'He was an odd boy. He wasn't a bad lot, but he was different from the others. Sometimes he would work all night long and then sleep all day. I've seen him go days on end without eating anything except the oranges that Madame Laure brought for him. He was affectionate to her. He loved her.'

'Did she seem jealous of the accused? Did you ever hear them argue?'

'Never. He was very worried about Madame Laure's health. She had a problem with her chest. That's what she died from in Switzerland a month after she went away.'

'And did you ever overhear any conversations, secrets, requests for money, perhaps, between Bernard Martin and the defendant?'

'Never. She never stayed long when she came. What I do remember, for example, what I noticed several times when I went into the room after she'd gone, was that the bed was still all made up. Now, maybe they must have worked it out some other way, don't you think?'

'Thank you; no need to go into detail,' said the Judge, as the crowd laughed.

Meanwhile, the accused woman, huddled on her bench, was overcome by nerves and started shaking. She was sobbing, and saying over and over again in despair, 'Have pity on me! Let me be. I killed him! Put me in prison, kill me, I deserve it! I deserve it a thousand times over; I deserve to be miserable and put to death, but why subject me to such shame? Yes, I killed him, I'm not asking for leniency, I just want it to be over, please let it be over . . .'

The hearing was adjourned until the next day. The crowd slowly dispersed. It was late; night was falling.

The summations would be heard the next day.

The accused woman was no longer of interest to anyone. She seemed to have lost all her beauty overnight, once and for all. She was an old, haggard woman. She was barely visible on the stand; she had left her hat on and lowered it to hide her face. The crowd only had eyes for Gladys Eysenach's Defence Counsel; he was still quite young with a scornful smirk and a beautiful mane of dark hair. He was the star of the day.

Meanwhile, she listened to the prosecution's summation, her face hidden in her hands: 'Until the night of 24 December 1934, the woman whom you see before you, gentlemen of the jury, was a member of life's privileged classes. She was still beautiful, in good health, freely enjoying a considerable fortune. Nevertheless, from her early childhood she had no family, no home, no example of morality. Ah! If only she had been fortunate enough to be born into a respectable middle-class family . . .'

The accused woman slowly let her hands fall on to her knees. She raised her face for a moment; it was pale and tense. She continued listening.

'A poor woman, an ignorant woman, an abused woman would perhaps have deserved leniency. But this woman . . .

'I implore the gentlemen of the jury not to allow the flame of justice to be extinguished. You must prove that justice exists for everyone, that if the charm, the beauty, the sophistication of this woman must be taken into account, they must be placed on the scales of justice in order to cause them to weigh heavily on the side of harshness. This woman committed murder. Her act was premeditated. She deserves a punishment that is proportionate to her crime.'

Next came the wonderful summation of the defence. Every now and again his biting voice turned sweet, almost feminine. The lawyer portrayed Gladys as a woman who had lived only for love, who cared for nothing in the world but love, and who deserved, in the name of love, to forget and to be forgiven; he spoke of the terrible demon of sensuality who lies in wait for ageing women, pushing them towards misdeeds and shame. The women in the courtroom were crying.

The Judge then turned towards Gladys and asked the traditional question: 'Does the accused have anything she wishes to add?'

Gladys remained silent for a long time. Finally, she shook her head and replied, 'No. Nothing.' Then, she added quietly, 'I am not asking for leniency. I committed a terrible crime . . .'

It was a warm, stormy evening, shot through with the dazzling rays of the setting sun; the atmosphere in the courtroom was nearly suffocating, and the observers grew more and more nervous and worked up. A muffled hum ran through the crowd, predicting the forthcoming verdict. The jury had retired and the accused woman had been led out.

Towards nine o'clock in the evening a bell finally rang, so low that it could hardly be heard; it marked the end of the jury's deliberation. Night had fallen. In the courtroom, packed to capacity, steam seemed to rise from the crowd and form condensation on the closed windows; the heat was unbearable.

The foreman of the jury, pale, his hands shaking, read out the responses to the questions. The Judge announced the verdict. A murmur ran through the press box and the people standing in the public gallery: 'Five years in prison . . .'

The spectators filed out of the doors of the ancient Law Courts. As they walked outside, everyone stopped at the entrance to breathe in the cool wind; it was raining again, in large, irregular drops.

'It'll rain again tomorrow,' someone said, pointing at the sky.

'Let's go for a beer,' said someone else.

Two women were talking about their husbands. The wind carried their words towards the dark, peaceful Seine.

Just as people forget the actors as soon as a play is over, so no one gave Gladys Eysenach another thought.

She had played her part. It had been a rather banal part, in the end. A crime of passion ... A somewhat modest sentence ... What would become of her? No one cared about her future; no one cared about her past.

1

Gladys may have been older and in decline, but she was still beautiful. Time had touched her reluctantly, with a careful, gentle hand. It had scarcely altered the shape of her face: her every feature seemed lovingly sculpted, tenderly caressed. Her long white neck remained untouched; only her eyes, which nothing could make younger, no longer sparkled as before. The expression in her eyes betrayed the anxious wisdom and weariness of age, but when she lowered them, everyone watching her could see the young girl who had danced for the first time at the Melbournes' ball in London, one beautiful June evening so very long ago.

In the Melbournes' reception room, with its pale wood panelling and hard window seats upholstered in red damask, narrow mirrors set into the panelling had reflected a slim young girl, still somewhat awkward and rather shy; she had golden hair that fell in a fringe on to her pale forehead and sparkling dark eyes. No one knew who she was: her name was Gladys Burnera.

She wore long gloves, a white dress whose skirt was decorated with chiffon, and a corsage of fresh roses; a wide satin belt showed off her waist; when she danced, she looked as if happiness were lifting her off the ground, as if a gust of wind might carry her away; her hair, literally the colour of gold, was plaited and wound round her head in a crown; no doubt she was wearing it that way for the first time: she paused in front of every mirror, tilted her head and looked at her pale, slender neck, completely bare, without even a delicate gold chain. A little bouquet of small red roses, richly coloured and sweet-smelling, her favourite flowers, was tucked into her belt at the waist; every now and again she would close her eyes to breathe in their perfume, and she knew that she would never, ever forget that scent of roses in the warm ballroom, the feel of the night breeze on her shoulders, the brilliant lights, the waltz that lingered in her ears. She was so very happy. No, not happy, not yet, but it was the expectation of happiness, the heavenly desire and passionate thirst for happiness, that filled her heart.

Only yesterday she had been the powerless, sad child of a mother she detested. Today she looked like a woman, beautiful, admired, soon to be loved. 'Loved,' she thought and immediately felt profound anxiety: she believed herself ugly, poorly dressed, badly educated; her gestures became brusque and awkward: fearfully she looked around for her cousin, Teresa Beauchamp, who was sitting with the other mothers. But gradually, dancing made her feel giddy; her blood ran faster, burning through her veins; she turned her head, studied the trees in the private park, the warm, humid night illuminated by yellow lights, the white columns in the ballroom, as slender and elegant as the young women. Everything was bewitching; everything looked beautiful to her, rare and enchanting; life took on a new flavour she had never tasted before: it was bitter-sweet.

Until she was eighteen years old, she had lived with her mother, a cold woman, harsh and virtually mad, an elderly painted doll who was sometimes frivolous and sometimes terrifying, who dragged her Persian cats, her daughter, her restlessness, all over the world.

As she danced that evening at the Melbournes' home, she was haunted by the image of that small, dried-out, cold woman with her green eyes. The two months she could spend in London with the Beauchamps would pass so quickly . . . She shook her head; she dismissed such thoughts and danced more lightly, more quickly; her skirts swayed around her and their swaying light chiffon gave her a delightful feeling of giddiness.

She would never, ever forget that brief summer. Never would she recapture that unique feeling of joy. Deep within everyone's heart there always remains a sense of longing for that hour, that summer, that one brief moment of blossoming. For several weeks or months, rarely longer, a beautiful young woman lives outside ordinary life. She is intoxicated. She feels as if she exists beyond time, beyond its laws; she experiences, not the monotonous succession of days passing by, but moments of intense, almost desperate happiness. And so she danced, she ran, through the Beauchamps' gardens at dawn, and then suddenly she felt that she'd been sleepwalking, that she was already half awake, that the dream was over.

Her cousin, Teresa Beauchamp, did not understand such passion, such *joie de vivre* that at times was transformed into moments of deep sadness. Teresa had always been more fragile, cooler. She was a few years older than Gladys. She was thin, slight; she had the physique of a fifteen-year-old girl, a delicate little head with skin pulled rather tightly across her temples, a yellowish complexion, beautiful dark eyes and a soft, wheezing voice that betrayed the early signs of the damage caused by the pulmonary condition from which she suffered.

She had married a Frenchman, but since she had been born and raised in England, she always spent time there; she owned a beautiful house in London. Teresa's childhood had been happy, her adolescence exemplary; she had been introduced into high society gradually, but Gladys had been thrown into it suddenly, all at once. Teresa had never been as beautiful as Gladys; no man had ever looked at her the way they looked at this gauche young girl.

When they arrived at the Melbournes', Gladys had grabbed Teresa's hand and squeezed it like a terrified child. Now she was dancing; she moved past Teresa without seeing her, a sweet, triumphant smile on her beautiful lips. Teresa, who felt tired after just one waltz, looked enviously at Gladys, admiring the delicate frame that hid nerves of steel. Yet, whenever she was asked 'Isn't your little cousin beautiful?' she would slowly nod her head with the surprised, weary gesture that made her look as graceful as an injured bird, then give a measured reply: 'She has the makings of a great beauty', for women do not see how the fleeting and almost terrifying radiance of beauty will fade from the faces of their peers.

'*Nous essayons de la distraire*,' she said, first in French. 'We're trying to give her a good time.'

She sat up even straighter on the hard cushions of the settee; she never leaned against the back of furniture; she never showed signs of impatience. She had unhealthily bright cheeks; she smiled nervously, wearily, and slowly fanned herself. It was getting late; she felt overwhelmed by profound sadness. At first it had given her pleasure to watch Gladys with the indulgent affection of the older woman; but now, she didn't know why, it was painful to see her so beautiful, so full of life; at one point she felt as if she wanted to grab her by the arm and shout, 'Enough. Stop. You are too dazzling, too happy.'

She had no idea that for many years to come Gladys would arouse the same envious sadness in the hearts of all women.

Teresa felt ashamed; she fanned herself more quickly. She was wearing a satin dress of a dullish bronze colour with a double lace skirt; its bodice was embroidered with chenille leaves and bronze pearls. She looked at herself in the mirror and thought she was ugly; she desperately, hopelessly envied Gladys's simple white dress and golden hair. She reminded herself that she was married, happy, that she had a son, that this little Gladys was at the threshold of an uncertain future.

'Go on then, my darling, you too will change one day ... such daring, such youth: how quickly they are lost, and the triumphant way you look at everyone, that will also fade away. You'll have children, grow old. You still don't know what is in store for you, my poor darling.'

Suddenly she stood up and walked over to Gladys, who was standing in front of the red curtain of a window. She touched her shoulder with her fan. 'We have to go home now, darling, come along . . .'

Gladys turned towards her. Teresa was shocked by the change that a single hour of pleasure had made to this docile, quiet young girl. Gladys's every gesture was made with great ease and sylphlike grace; her expression was triumphant, her laughter joyful and mocking. She seemed barely to hear what Teresa was saying.

'Oh, no, Tess,' she said, impatiently shaking her head, 'no, please, Tess . . .'

'Yes, darling . . .'

'One more hour, just one.'

'No, darling, it's late; imagine staying up all night, at your age . . .'

'One more dance then, just one more dance . . .'

Tess sighed; her breathing became more irregular, more painful, as always when she was tired or irritated; she was wheezing.

'I was also eighteen once, Gladys,' she said, 'and not that long ago. I understand that you find the ball wonderful, but you must learn how to leave pleasure behind before it leaves you behind. It's late. Haven't you had a good enough time?'

'Yes, but now it's over,' Gladys murmured in spite of herself.

'Tomorrow you will be pale and tired because you didn't want to go home when you should. This isn't the last ball you'll go to; summer isn't over yet.'

'But it will be over soon,' said Gladys, and her wide dark eyes sparkled with desire and despair.

'Well, then, that will be the time to cry, and you know

very well that everything must come to an end. You must
learn how to resign yourself to things.'

Gladys lowered her head, but she wasn't listening; a
voice rose from deep within her heart, a primitive and
passionate voice, blocking out all those pointless words,
a cruel, powerful voice that shouted, 'Leave me alone! I
want my pleasure! Deny me a single one of my pleasures
and I'll hate you! If you interfere with a single second of
happiness that God has granted me, I'll wish you were
dead.'

All she could hear was that intoxicating fanfare, the
voice of youth itself. Was it possible that she would see
this night end, watch it disappear into the void, the past?
This night – so beautiful, so perfect – to others was nothing
more than another summer's ball in London, 'a tiresome
affair', as Tess put it, no more than a few hours, soon to
be forgotten . . .

'Come along now, I say,' Tess said, almost harshly.

Gladys looked at her with surprise.

'I don't feel well; I'm tired. We have to go home . . .'

'I'm sorry,' murmured Gladys, taking her hand.

Her face had changed; once again it was childlike and
innocent; the cruel passion in her eyes had disappeared.

'Let's go,' said Tess, forcing herself to smile. 'You're a
good, sensible girl. Come along . . .'

Gladys followed her without saying a word.

2

To Gladys, the last ball of that summer was a whirl of dancing, sound and colour that caught her up for a few hours then abandoned her, throwing her back down to earth feeling weary and disappointed. She had to leave the next day.

She returned to the Beauchamps' house at dawn. A milky fog lit up London; the pale, glistening streets were empty; the morning was almost cold, and the breeze left the taste of rain and damp coal on the lips, though now and again wafts of scent filled the air from the roses blossoming in the parks.

Gladys slowly touched her face; her cheeks burned as if on fire. She could feel her heart beating quickly, anxiously, to the rhythm of the last waltz she had danced. She hummed it absent-mindedly, gently stroked her hair, leaned towards Tess and laughed, but she was sad. It was always the same: her joy suddenly disappeared and left her feeling deeply, bitterly melancholy. She dreamily thought about a handsome gentleman she had found attractive and with whom all the young women had fallen in love that summer. He was a young Polish man who worked at the Russian Embassy; his name was Count Tarnovsky. She thought of all the beautiful women she had seen and the fortunate young girls whose lives were already mapped out for them, while she had barely any social status, she who was the daughter of divorced parents, the daughter of Sophie Burnera, 'an unhappy woman, a wicked woman', as Tess called her. She looked over at her cousin who was sitting beside her and felt sorry for her: she seemed so frail, so tired, so ill; every now and again she would cough painfully. Claude Beauchamp had closed the car window and turned towards the two women. She smiled at him shyly, but he didn't seem to notice her.

He had a long, delicate face and thin cheeks, as if he were drawing them into his mouth beneath his cheekbones; his beautiful mouth had fine lips that formed almost a single straight line across his face when they were closed. He was very tall and not very strong looking, and he normally stood hunched over with his head slightly forward. He was polite, cold, reserved and quiet. He was young, but to Gladys he seemed nearly an old man. She admired him but had never set out to be attractive to him.

The car stopped in front of the Beauchamps' house. Downstairs, in Claude's library, some drinks had been set out. It was a cold house; the fires were always lit when Teresa was to get home late. A few logs were still burning, lighting up the very tall old furniture: it was old-fashioned, made of antique dark wood, polished as brightly as ebony.

Gladys opened the window and sat down in front of it.

'You'll catch cold, darling,' Tess said with a sigh.

'No I won't,' murmured Gladys.

'At least throw a coat over your shoulders.'

'No, no, my love, I'm not afraid of the cold, I'm not afraid of anything in this world.'

Both women had the Victorian English habit of addressing each other in affectionate terms. They only ever called each other 'darling', 'my sweetheart', 'my love . . .'. They smiled at each other when saying these words, but their eyes were harsh.

Gladys took the flowers from her belt and breathed in their scent.

Tess made an angry gesture. 'Leave them alone,' she said, 'they've wilted.'

'That doesn't matter. Only these little red roses manage to wilt the way they should: they don't wither away, they burn from within. Look,' she said, showing her the flowers in her hand, 'smell them, what a delicious perfume . . .'

She held them to Teresa's nose but she turned her head away. 'The smell of flowers makes me feel ill,' she said sadly.

Gladys smiled; she felt ashamed; she could see she was upsetting Tess. 'Poor little Teresa,' she thought. She felt sorry for her, but she also felt a restless cruelty, the desire to know, to calculate the extent of her power as a woman for the first time. Her small face was pale from staying up all night, tense and trembling.

'What am I doing?' she suddenly thought, 'and why?'

They heard the voice of a child waking up from the floor above; it was Olivier, the Beauchamps' little boy. Teresa immediately stood up. 'Six o'clock already. Olivier's getting up . . .'

'Don't go to him now; go and get some rest.'

Teresa picked up her fan from the chair and left the room. Claude and Gladys were alone. Gladys opened the balcony doors. 'It's so light out . . .'

Claude switched off the lamp. They went outside and stood on the stone balcony that ran round the entire house. It was a very beautiful morning, very quiet; they could hear birds singing in the garden next door, the sharp, joyous, intoxicating songs that welcome the sunlight.

'Aren't you tired?'

'Not at all,' she replied impatiently. 'You too, Claude, all you ever talk about is being tired, getting some rest. Don't you find that staying up all night makes you feel as light as air? It's as if you're no longer made of flesh and blood, as if a gust of wind could carry you away . . .'

'Look,' he said, 'look at how that tree is swaying in the wind.'

'Yes, it's beautiful.'

She leaned over the balcony, half closed her eyes to feel the morning wind brush against her eyelids. 'This is the most beautiful time of day . . .'

'Yes,' he said, looking at her. 'The only two moments of any real value, "worth considering",' he said in English, 'are the birth and death of things, the beginning and the end.'

'I don't understand,' Gladys said suddenly, her voice low and passionate, 'I don't understand why the old man in that book you like so much insists that he's never once in his whole life been able to say, "Stand still!"'

'Oh, because he was an old fool, I imagine.'

She smiled and breathed in the wind, tilted her lovely head, looked at her bare arm. 'Time,' she said softly, 'stand still.'

'Yes,' he whispered.

She laughed, but he was watching her with an intense, passionate expression. He seemed less to admire her than to fear and almost hate her.

'Gladys . . .' he said at last.

He said her name again with a kind of astonishment, then leaned over and took her hand: it was still the hand of a child, thin and unadorned, hiding among the folds of her dress. He kissed it, trembling. He kissed her slim arm that still had traces of bumps and scratches, for she was sometimes rough, like a tomboy, and she loved difficult horses, obstacles, danger. He stood bowed before her, as humble as a child. Gladys would never, ever forget that moment, the intoxicating arrogance and divine satisfaction that filled her heart.

'This,' she mused, 'this is happiness.'

She didn't pull away her hand; only her delicate nostrils flared slightly and her youthful face suddenly transformed into the face of a woman, a face that was cunning, greedy and cruel. How wonderful it was to see a man at her feet. Was there anything better in this world than the dawn of her power as a woman? It was this she had been waiting for, this she had sensed was about to happen for so many days now. Pleasure, dancing, success: all these things paled into insignificance before this stinging sensation, this kind of biting she felt within her now.

'Is this love?' she mused. 'Oh, no! It was the pleasure of being loved . . . it was almost sacrilegious . . .'

'I'm only a child,' she said, 'and you are Tess's husband.'

He looked up at her and smiled. They watched each other for a moment.

'A child, yes . . .' he said painfully, 'but already a jaded, dangerous flirt . . .'

His face had become impassive again. Only his hands were shaking. He wanted to leave, but she asked him quietly, 'Are you in love with me, then?'

He didn't reply; his thin lips took the shape of that pale, straight line that cut across his face and which she knew so well.

'He'll give in,' she thought and she felt a desire to re-create that sensation of sharp, strange, almost physical joy.

'Answer me,' she said, touching his hand. 'Say it: "I love you", even if it isn't true. I've never heard anyone say those words. I want to hear them. I want to hear you say them, Claude. Tell me . . .'

'I love you,' he said.

She pulled away from him with a weary, happy little laugh. That moment of piercing desire had passed; she felt a kind of shame combined with pleasure; she slowly lowered her beautiful eyes, moved away from the trembling arms that wished to clasp her to him and smiled.

'No,' she said, 'what's the point? *I* don't love you . . .'

He walked away and left the room without looking at her.

3

Some time later, while travelling, Gladys happened to meet Count Tarnovsky again, the young Polish man who had pleased her at a London ball. She married him and lived with him for two years. He was handsome and as vain about his good looks as a young girl; he was unfaithful, a liar, affectionate and weak. Their married life was unbearable to both of them, because they used the same feminine weapons against each other: lies, ruses and whims. Afterwards, she could not forgive him for having made her suffer; she hated suffering; like children, she expected and demanded to be happy.

After they separated she met Richard Eysenach, a famous financier of dubious origins and President of the Mexican Petroleum Company. He was feared for his sharp, ruthless intelligence. He was ugly, with a heavy, powerful body, muscular arms and a wide forehead that was partially hidden by his thick black hair. Beneath his full eyebrows his piercing green eyes would stare at a rival, scrutinising him with scornful, amused tolerance. He only found women attractive if they were beautiful, docile and knew how to keep quiet. He trained Gladys to obey him, to appear happy and cheerful when he looked at her a certain way, to think of nothing in life apart from being beautiful and finding pleasure. He never grew tired of watching her getting dressed, choosing slowly between two pieces of jewellery, studying her features in the mirror. He found sharp, sensual pleasure in treating her like a child. When she pressed herself against him, when she whispered 'I'm so small compared to you, so weak . . .', when she looked at him in a certain way, raising her sweet, mocking face towards him, a flash of desire and almost madness shot across his cold, impassive face. Then he would throw himself on top of her, passionately biting her lips, calling her 'My little girl, my sweet child, my little one . . .'

This unspoken vice that was appeased through her was the source of pleasure for both of them and, for Gladys, the secret of the power that she wielded over him and over others. She loved it when he caressed her roughly, savagely. Later in life, all the men she would find attractive resembled Richard in some way. For a long time she had a lover, Sir Mark Forbes, the English statesman who was very famous just before the war. He was hard and ambitious, educated to follow a routine and with a love of power; but with her he was lonely, weak and defenceless. That was what she liked; that was what annoyed him; she constantly had to prove to herself that she could dominate men.

In the years preceding the war her beauty attained the point of perfection that only happiness and the fulfilment of every desire can bring about in a woman. Olivier Beauchamp, the son of Claude and Teresa, met her when she was passing through Paris. It was 1907 and he was barely out of adolescence. He saw a woman whose face and body were as beautiful as they had been when she was twenty, but who exuded the air of self-confidence and peace that comes from happiness. She was surrounded by men who were in love with her. She had become as accustomed to promises, pleading and tears as a drunkard was to wine; she never had enough and such sweet poison was so essential to her that she would not have been able to live without it. She made no secret of it. She believed that a real woman is never blasé, but rather an indefatigable little creature: an ambitious man might grow weary of accolade and a miser of gold, but a real woman could never forsake her femininity; when she thought about growing old, it seemed so far away that she could consider it without fear, imagining that death would come to her before her life of pleasure was over.

Meanwhile, her daughter, little Marie-Thérèse, was growing up. She was a beautiful little girl with a pale, fresh complexion, long straight blonde hair and the touching gracefulness of an age when beauty is not yet found in one's expression but in the shape of the features, the texture of the skin; it is a time of life when the flickering in the eyes and at the corners of the mouth announce the future blossoming of emotions rather than emotions themselves. 'She'll never look like her mother,' people said, 'never be her mother's equal.' She lived in the shadow of her beautiful mother and, like everyone else who knew Gladys, she strove only to please her, to serve her, to love her.

4

In 1914 Gladys lived near Antibes in a beautiful but uncomfortable house, built in the Italian style; it had belonged to the Counts Dolcebuone and was named 'Sans-Souci'.

'I only rented it because of its name, 'Care-free', for it encapsulates all of life's wisdom,' she would say.

The rooms were vast and cold, the furniture covered in threadbare red damask. But the dark walls softened the glaring light of the Midi and Gladys liked that. Every day, just after she woke up, she would pick up her mirror and study her features, and she would find pleasure in the glowing shadow that softly lit up her face.

Spring was just beginning; it was warm but a wind blew in from the mountains, a swift, biting wind.

On that morning in March, Gladys got up late and, as usual, before she had properly opened her eyes her hand automatically reached for the mirror. Ever since she had become a woman, this was her first gesture, her first thought when she woke up. For a long while she studied her face affectionately. The golden colour of her hair had darkened slightly; it was now that pale, light colour that was then called 'ash'. She pushed back her dishevelled hair with one hand and tilted her long white neck. Her wide dark eyes seemed always to smile with a kind of secret amusement when she looked at her admirers, but when she was alone they grew sadder and deeper, clouded over, and her dilated, pulsating pupils made her eyes look strange and anxious.

Gladys was, and always would be, profoundly aware of her beauty. At every moment of every day she felt it was her inner peace. Her life was uncomplicated: get dressed, be attractive, meet with a lover, change clothes, be attractive ... Sometimes she would think, 'I'm forty years old.' Before the war that was a terrible age to be, the 'upper limit'. Women like her, whose beauty had remained intact at forty, were rare.

At such thoughts she would immediately frown and force herself to forget. She was so beautiful ... It was so easy to forget ...

She opened the shutters; the roses were swaying in the wind. She started to dress and complete her long, meticulous beauty regime.

Women came to see her, then left. She was always surrounded by women who, each and every one of them, were no more than a pale imitation of her, who copied her dresses, her whims, her smiles. Gladys loved this circle of painted faces that leaned so eagerly towards her, the jingling of jewellery as they followed her, their bright, false faces, full of envy and hatred, on which she could read a compliment even more easily than in the eyes of the men in love with her. Secretly they studied how she moved. They tried to bend their stiff bodies, held tightly in their corsets, with the nonchalant grace of Gladys. They moved in a herd from Cannes to Monte Carlo, turned up at Mimi Meyendorf's, then at Clara Mackay's or Nathalie Esslenko's. All they thought about was stealing men from each other, and especially from Gladys Eysenach, the richest and happiest of all of them. They chattered, laughed, babbled, leaned forward lightly to kiss Gladys's cheek.

'My darling, my dear Gladys, how beautiful you looked last night . . .'

Large hats decorated with roses, held in place with gold pins, bobbed up and down all around Gladys. Tall Louis XV canes, the fad that summer, echoed against the paving stones of Sans-Souci.

Gladys looked at her women friends and smiled, half closing her beautiful eyes; sometimes she reproached herself for the rather base pleasure she took from having these women around her. 'But they do so amuse me,' she thought.

That day, when Gladys was ready, Lily Ferrer came in. She was Bavarian and had an unpleasant husky accent; she was tall and massive; her face was so plastered with make-up that it looked like a mask. Gladys liked her best: she felt towards women who were older than she was an extreme indulgence and affectionate pity.

They kissed. They sometimes spoke of intimate things, but in the way that women do: whimsically, frivolously, instinctively hiding their most secret thoughts yet revealing them, in spite of themselves, through a gibe or a sigh, using their light-hearted words to cover up some bitter experience that wafted through their vain words like the scent of incense or salt.

They started talking about the ball they'd attended the previous evening.

'Nathalie drove me mad for a week wanting to know what dress and jewellery I'd be wearing,' Gladys told her, laughing. 'She's just a little gold-digger from Central Europe who got herself a husband because he was off guard! And oh how it shows! Since I didn't want to tell her, she thought I'd be covered in fabulous precious stones and wearing my Golconda jewellery, so she threw on everything she owned. She was flashing like one of those jewel-studded gilt boxes that hold the relics of saints.' Gladys smiled as she thought of her white dress and bare arms, without any jewellery whatsoever, her hands with no rings, and the murderous look Nathalie had flashed her, crushed beneath her diamond armour. 'Are you enjoying the social scene this summer?'

'It's deadly dull. But Gladys, where else would you go?'

'I don't know. But I want to leave. I've been feeling sad for some time now, weary. I feel a kind of cruel restlessness,' she said lightly, trying to find the right words, then slowly shrugging her shoulders. 'Yes, that's the way I feel . . .'

'But why?' asked Lily Ferrer, screwing up her eyes. 'Are you in love with someone?'

'Oh, Lord no! I'm faithful to Mark.'

Lily Ferrer nodded. 'Men who loved you when you were twenty, and who continue to see you the way you looked then are impossible to replace.'

'Yes,' said Gladys.

She thought that she would never forget, never be able to replace Richard. He had died two years before; that day, her life had changed for ever. Why? Ah! It was . . .

impossible to put into words. At first, she hadn't understood the depth of her loss. She had thought, 'Mark . . .' But no, nothing could replace Richard. They had spent their whole life together, on ships and in hotel suites. He had died in New York, in a room at the Plaza, soon after they had arrived. He had come into her room in the middle of the night, while she was asleep, and leaned over the bed. Waking with a start, she had seen his pale face coming closer and, for the very first time, a look of gentle weakness in his eyes. She recalled the noise of New York beneath their windows, the regular flashes of harsh light that shone through the curtains like the beacon of a lighthouse.

'Don't call anyone,' he'd said. 'This is the end.'

He had murmured something else as she took him in her arms for his very last kiss: 'My poor darling, poor darling . . .'

She hadn't understood then. She had grabbed his hand, but it was stiff; he was dead. Happiness is such a terrible gift when it is the kind of happiness that is too complete, too daring, and which ends, as all things must. From that day on she had begun to sense, through discreet little signs, that for her the light of day would falter and gradually fade away.

A few months after his death, she had been astonished to learn that he'd had a mistress throughout their entire marriage; she was an elderly actress, his confidante in his financial and political dealings. In his Will he requested that Gladys provide an allowance to this woman and she had scrupulously carried out his wishes. Yes, he had been unfaithful to her and she had also been unfaithful, but she had been happy with him. She would never be as happy with anyone else.

She sighed and looked sadly out at the garden. Dark little roses were growing beneath her window. She smiled at them. She loved roses.

'What do you think of those new coloured wigs?' Lily Ferrer asked.

'They're so hideous! Did you see the one that Laure was wearing last night, the aubergine one? Why did the Bilibines leave?'

'They lost money gambling.'

'I think that women who love gambling are happy,' said Gladys.

'Happy? Why bring up happiness? You're happy, Gladys,' the old woman said, sighing, 'but you don't know it yet. You'll see, when you're my age. When all is said and done, there is only one truth, only one kind of happiness, and that is youth. How old are you? Surely no more than thirty? Well, you've got ten years of happiness left. Forty is a terrible enough age. After that, well, I'd say that you adapt, you become less demanding. You enjoy the little pleasures of life,' she said, sighing, thinking of her lover. 'But when you're forty you don't realise you're getting old. You live in the illusion that you're only twenty, that you will be twenty for all of eternity, then suddenly it hits you. It can be anything: a word, a look in some man's eyes, a child who wants to get married, oh, it's horrible . . .'

Gladys shivered and tried to hide it by forcing herself to laugh.

'Do what I do. Don't count the years as they pass and they will only mark you lightly.'

'Do you think so?' the woman murmured doubtfully.

'I want to go to Rome,' Gladys said suddenly, 'let's go together.'

'What about Sir Mark? How could you want to leave Sir Mark when he's only just arrived?'

'He'll go where I go.'

'How do you do it, my dear? How do you manage to keep men on a lead the way you do, as if they were puppies? I was young once too, and beautiful,' she said, turning away from the large mirror, 'and love brought me nothing but unhappiness. But what else is there in this world?'

'I dislike being in love,' said Gladys quietly.

'But darling, then why . . . ?'

'Why Sir Mark?'

'Sir Mark and the others . . .'

'There are no others,' said Gladys.

'Come now,' whispered the older woman in the warm, secret, sensual and sad tone of voice women use to speak of love when love is coming to an end for them.

'Really,' said Gladys, smiling.

She slowly powdered her bare arms.

'Life is sad, when all is said and done, don't you think? There are only moments of exhilaration, of passion . . . Like when you stand on a balcony at night and listen to some sweet, enchanting music. Or when you dance. Ah! I can't explain it, but that's what people are trying to find, that's what true happiness is.'

A woman came in carrying a stack of sable furs over her arm; she briskly shook them out. She sold beauty products and was called Carmen Gonzales; Gladys had known her for many years: everywhere that Gladys went, a circle of masseuses, hairdressers and make-up women immediately surrounded her.

Carmen Gonzales was old, short and stocky, with a rough, gloomy face; she had on a threadbare black satin dress that clung tightly to her hips and a black straw hat that sat awkwardly on top of her head.

Gladys greeted her graciously. Gladys was always sweet and charming, and people took pleasure in serving her. But even with her, Gonzales retained the harsh, defiant expression that inspired respectful fear in her clients. She had courage, the kind of fierce bravery of the working classes who, whenever they feel tired and unhappy, grit their teeth and work even harder; she was a masseuse and a midwife, but she also supplied beauty products. Sometimes, during a massage, in a rare moment of effusiveness, she would stand up straight and sigh; her bare arm would wipe away the sweat from her brow with the same gesture a laundress might use. Then her face would light up with a fleeting smile and she would think, 'What can any of *you* know about life? *I've* seen it all . . .'

She lived in three little rooms that smelled of herbs and camphor, and was filled from morning to night by veiled women who waited their turn and pretended not to notice each other. She wore rings that dug into the flesh of her thick, agile hands, but she knew how to transform all their tired faces, how to mould them, make their wrinkles disappear, how to create a deceptive mask out of their old flesh.

She bought dresses, jewellery and furs from courtesans

who had gambled away everything, and sold them to her regular clients.

When Gladys saw the sable pelts, she shook her head and gently held Carmen at bay. 'No, I don't want to buy anything, no.'

'Just have a look,' said the old woman.

Gladys had turned away and was talking to Lily Ferrer.

'Do speak to George,' Lily was begging her quietly. 'Make him understand that he is killing me. There is a limit to a woman's patience. He's not evil, but he's so nonchalant, so cruel. He's tempted by every woman he sees.'

'Come on, now,' whispered Gladys, slowly shrugging her lovely shoulders. 'Lily! You must be more sensible than that. What's the point of letting yourself suffer?'

The old woman sighed. 'Love,' she said, and a tear rolled down her painted cheek.

'He cares for you very much.' She took Lily's hands in hers. 'Darling, listen to me . . .'

She enjoyed talking about love, hearing secret confidences, wiping away tears. She knew how to console, appease, flatter. Love was the only thing she was interested in; everything else made her feel nothing more than gracious indifference.

Lily finally seemed calmer. Gladys left her alone and went to see Carmen, who was waiting in the next room.

'Are you interested?' asked Carmen, pointing to the sable furs.

Gladys slowly stroked the beautiful pelts. 'No, I don't need any new furs. But they are beautiful . . .'

'They belonged to Celina Meller,' said Carmen, naming

an old courtesan who had been famous in the past. 'They're a set of furs that a lover gave her from Russia, a long time ago. She had a beautiful outfit made for the balls, but she had to sell it six months ago. These are the few that were left, which she wanted to use to have other outfits made. They must be sold now, along with everything else she owns. This one would make a very beautiful collar for your velvet cape, the white one.'

'Celina Meller?' murmured Gladys. 'Is she that poor, then?'

'Oh, yes! She's got nothing left.'

'She was so beautiful, and that was only ten years ago.'

'Time goes fast at that age.'

'Poor woman,' said Gladys.

She had a sensitive, vivid imagination, but focused entirely on herself. Yet in a flash she imagined an old woman whose wrinkles made happier memories fade away.

'How much does she want for them?'

'Four thousand. It's a steal. But she has no choice. Everyone knows she needs money and is offering her half that.'

'All right, then. Leave them here. I'll buy them to help her out, the poor woman.'

'All right,' said Carmen in her gloomy voice. 'You're getting a bargain; I know what I'm talking about.'

Lily came in to find them.

'Come and have lunch with me, Gladys,' she said. 'That way you'll get to see him,' she added more quietly.

'Oh, I can't, darling, I promised my little daughter I'd have lunch with her. She complains that she never sees me and she's right.'

'You're lucky to have a little girl,' Lily Ferrer said, sighing.

She looked at the picture of the child in a gold frame that sat on the table. 'She'll be a beauty, but she won't have your figure.'

'She'll be more beautiful than me,' said Gladys affectionately.

She smiled at the adolescent face that seemed to look back at her with slight surprise and that strange and troubling seriousness of youth. It was a picture of Marie-Thérèse when she was thirteen: she had a small, delicate face, softly rounded, long straight blonde hair piled high on to the top of her head and held in place by a black bow.

The two women shook their heads.

'No, she'll never have your charm.'

'She's still a child, it's an awkward time of life,' said Gladys.

She sighed and smiled. Deep down in her heart, she couldn't admit how old Marie-Thérèse really was, not even to herself. Eighteen. She was already a woman. She preferred to say and let people think: 'Fifteen . . . nearly fifteen . . .'

All the women she knew did the same. They knocked off one, two or three years from the age of those children they weren't able to hide away and, little by little, they themselves forgot the child's real age, thus satisfying their delusions of themselves as both women and mothers. Gladys didn't notice her daughter was growing up. When she spoke to her or looked at her, her mind re-created the features of a young girl of fifteen, who no longer existed except in her imagination.

'I've brought you your rouge for tonight,' said Carmen, taking some make-up out of an old bag.

'Ah!' said Gladys and her lovely face grew attentive.

She went over to the mirror, put some rouge on her cheek and dusted it with powder.

'Yes, that's better. Don't you think? The other one was too light. A darker colour is better under the light.'

She turned round slowly, looking into the mirror with intense seriousness. Then her lips parted in a sweet, triumphant smile. 'That's good . . . Yes, it's good.'

Carmen, however, was on her way out. Lily and Gladys – who was finally ready – followed her and slowly walked through the garden. Near the road the air held the scent of sweet roses, petrol and the clean, cool smell of the mountains. The two women got into the car and headed for Nice.

5

To Gladys, the years had passed with the swiftness of a dream. As she aged, they felt shorter and seemed to fly by more quickly, but the days felt long. Certain moments were heavy and bitter. She didn't like being alone: as soon as the chatter of women ceased around her, as soon as the sound of words of love faded away, she felt deep anxiety within her heart.

For some time, now, everything had bored and irritated her. She turned away if she saw certain women in the street. The beautiful little girls selling mimosa who ran barefoot through the dusty streets offended her with their carefree youth. She pushed them away with a harshness that surprised even her and made her feel ashamed. Sometimes she would call them back and give them some money, thinking, 'It's too hot here, oppressive, I'm bored . . .'

She was haunted by memories of her mother, whom she had detested; sometimes she pictured the curtains closed round the bed where Sophie Burnera slept in a morphine stupor. Then she would feel a kind of strange humiliation that nothing could pacify. She, Gladys

Eysenach, who was beautiful, admired, loved, still sometimes felt the sadness, the loneliness of her adolescence deep within her heart. If Richard were alive, she would have admitted that to him. But Richard was dead.

She would visit one friend after the other. With them, time would pass more quickly, but eventually she had to go home and still it was daytime. There was nothing left to do but try on dresses and visit the jewellers on the little sloping street near the public gardens, where the sea breeze blew in. Finally, night would come and she would feel as if she had been reborn. She would go home to Sans-Souci, get dressed, admire how she looked. How she loved doing that. Was there anything better in life, was there anything more sensual than being attractive? The desire to be alluring, to be loved – a commonplace pleasure that all women felt – to her became an obsession, similar to the profound way men felt about power or money, a thirst that increased with each passing year and that nothing could ever completely satisfy.

At last she was ready. She went into Marie-Thérèse's room and affectionately kissed her beautiful, pale cheeks; beneath the soft skin there was evidence of a passionate nature. She looked at her daughter lovingly. Marie-Thérèse remained so delightfully childlike, at least in her mother's eyes. Gladys dressed her in a way that made her more than an adolescent; she was the very symbol of adolescence: flat shoes, a long, straight, plain skirt, long hair that came down to her shoulders, a delicate gold chain round her neck; she was innocent and graceful.

'She only likes books, her dogs, running through the gardens,' thought Gladys. 'She's still so inexperienced and shy. I'll give it two or three more years and then I'll teach her. She'll dance and have fun. Oh! I won't be a cold, harsh mother. I'll be her friend; she'll tell me everything. She'll be happy. But it's too soon. She's still too young. She's shy, fragile. She mustn't be vain and frivolous, like me . . .'

To Marie-Thérèse she said, 'I don't know what I would have done if I'd had a daughter who was one of those unbearable little creatures who smoke and wear make-up and want to be like older women. But you, even the awkward phase hasn't spoiled you. You're still such an even-tempered little girl.'

Marie-Thérèse let her talk: she retained the great generosity of youth that so often and so oddly is combined with harshness. She realised how much her ageing mother was suffering. She had sensed it, understood it, even before Gladys herself became aware of it. She felt sorry for her. But, most especially, she felt so young, she could imagine such a long road before her, that she did not yet feel there was any rush to live.

She kissed her mother. 'How beautiful you look,' she said. 'You have a really lovely dress, my dear Mama. You are as beautiful as a fairy.'

And Gladys left for the ball, radiant and happy as in the past. She'd been to many other balls, the most brilliant in London and Paris, but she feared more than anything the unchanging social circle in England and France; every night you saw the same faces, you trotted out the same words, and for fifteen, twenty years at that . . .

Here, at least every summer brought a flood of new people.

That evening she had been invited to the Middletons in Cannes. She made her entrance; she smiled at the women who looked at her enviously. She sweetly nodded her divine little head with its ash-blonde hair. She basked in the kind of tranquillity that comes when passion is satisfied, that moment when the body reacts to excitement, its poison coursing through the body. She lowered her eyes with pity at the sight of the old women, those Fates dressed in velvet, their necks covered in diamond yokes; they pursed their lips and stared at her. She spotted Sir Mark Forbes. Not far from him sat his wife.

Lady Forbes was the daughter of the Duchess of Hereford; her great wealth and family name had served Sir Mark's political career well. She knew about her husband's affair, suffered because of it and fought it with all the redoubtable weapons of the betrayed wife, the most terrifying of which was the constant threat of divorce: it would have ruined Sir Mark. Caught between his wife and Gladys, Sir Mark's life was not a happy one. For several months, now, Gladys could sense within him an almost imperceptible resistance to her will, a coolness that worried and irritated her.

'He's sulking,' she thought, seeing that he did not rush up to greet her. 'Take your time, my handsome lover . . .'

Men surrounded her, asking her to dance. Among them was Olivier Beauchamp; she saw him often. Teresa had died some time before and Claude lived in Switzerland. Gladys invited Olivier to dinner, adding with gracious indifference, 'Marie-Thérèse likes you so much. You must come and see us more often.'

'Would you be happy to see someone from your past?'

'Who might that be?'

'My father.'

'Really? Is it possible he's finally going to leave Vevey?'

'Oh, no! I think he'll spend the rest of his life there. He says he couldn't live anywhere else. But he has to come to Paris on business and will spend a day here.'

'Well, that's good news.'

'Would you dance with me?' he asked.

She waltzed with him then, since the salon was so stifling, she went outside to sit on the terrace. She leaned over the stone balcony, still warm from the sunlight that day. It was late when she finally saw Sir Mark walking towards her.

'Has your wife left?' she asked.

'I've just taken her home and I came back to see you. Do you want to stay here a while longer?'

She half closed her beautiful eyes with weary, wonderful grace. 'Lord no! I'm tired . . .'

'Let's go, then.'

They left. It was nearly dawn.

'Gladys,' said Sir Mark, 'I have to talk to you . . .'

'Now? I want to go home. It's five o'clock.'

'Yes, now,' he murmured.

He got into the car with her. They drove slowly towards Antibes, along the coast road.

'Gladys,' he said, 'listen to me. If you see me as a friend, even if you no longer are in love with me the way you once were, you will take pity on me. I am exceedingly unhappy.'

'Oh, Mark,' she said, gently shrugging her shoulders.

'My wife . . .'

'I know, Mark, I know . . .'

She knew he was tormented by fear and his principles. He came from a poor Jewish family. He relied upon his wife's family for everything, but his wife was demanding that he leave Gladys, that he stop following her all over Europe, as he had done until now.

'I wouldn't survive a divorce,' he murmured painfully. 'Divorce is so scandalous in England. What am I to do, Gladys? My life is in your hands. I'm not young any more . . .'

'Don't be so silly,' she said softly.

She took his hand, leaned in close to him, but Sir Mark didn't pull away or seem anxious. He looked tired and ill. Disappointed, she let go of his hand and moved back. Wounded pride brought tears to her eyes. She turned her head, feeling somewhat ashamed. He was moved by this and thought how women rarely hide their sadness.

'What am I to do, Gladys?' he asked again.

'We've been in this situation ever since we met.'

'But it's becoming unbearable. I love you.'

She cut in, suddenly raised her hand to stop him; Sir Mark could see her fingers trembling. 'Don't say that.'

'Oh, Gladys! I was so in love with you.'

'Yes, you were. That's true. That's not a lie. You did love me, but I've hardly seen you at all this past year. You're cold, evasive, elusive. No, you don't love me any more.'

'Gladys, sooner or later life extinguishes even our most fervent passions. I'm tired, that's the truth of it; I can't fight a jealous woman any longer, her reproaches and suspicions. My children have adamantly taken their mother's side against me. You can't understand; your little girl adores you, but children you love so much can be such merciless judges.'

She wasn't listening to him; she lowered her head.

'Do you understand what I'm saying?' he whispered.

'Of course.'

'Gladys,' he said with sudden sincerity, 'I thought I would die before I'd ever leave you, but God has not granted me that blessing.'

'Your wife has won,' murmured Gladys.

'What difference does that make? My wife is only a symbol, a symbol of a certain type of peace that I deserve . . .'

'All you can think about is your own happiness.'

'Gladys, for so many years I've thought of nothing but you. And what did you give me in return? You let yourself be loved.'

She turned towards him, showing him the tears that flowed down her face, but he just looked at her sadly.

'Oh, Gladys! How like a woman. Because I finally have the strength to end it, you are starting to care about me. You'll soon regret having lost me.'

'I've always cared a great deal for you.'

'And I adored you. But you're so used to being adored . . . you are so supremely apathetic, so sweetly arrogant. How I loved you . . .'

'Oh! Don't talk to me like that,' she said, suddenly angry. 'It makes me feel as if I'm dead and you're crying over my grave. Why did you come to Nice? You shouldn't have come. You're as conservative in love as you are in politics, my darling. You treat love as if it were a ballet, with its set classical steps, the seduction scene, the passionate waltz, the allegro section when we quarrel . . . We are dancing the allegro. You should have said nothing, stopped writing to me, and it all would have been over. I would barely have noticed.'

'Will you miss me, Gladys?'

'Why are you going?' she said without answering his question. 'Why are you leaving me? There's something you're not telling me. Are you in love with another woman? Just say so and you'll free me from my most terrifying thought.'

'What is that?'

'Have I grown old, Mark?' she asked suddenly, and immediately suppressed a gesture of anxiety and fear.

('Why did I say that?' she thought. 'It isn't true . . . I'm young, young!')

He shook his head. 'I don't know. Do you think that men look at the face of the woman they love? They look further, deeper than her features. They think: "Will she hurt me more today than yesterday? Will she finally grow bored with making me suffer? Will she ever love me?" You see, even when madly in love, we think only of ourselves.'

They had arrived. The dawn light lit up the house. He walked a few steps with her down the path. She was suffering from a kind of pain she had never felt before. But she was no fool. She knew very well it wasn't love. She had never felt anything other than the all-consuming desire to be loved, the delicious satisfaction of pride fulfilled. She looked and him and thought, 'If I kiss him, if he takes me in his arms, holds me tightly . . . No, I'm above that. I want him to go. I'm beautiful, I'm young, someone else will come along . . .'

She held out her hand to him. 'Goodbye, Mark.'

He was trembling. At that moment she understood her power over him and her defeat, for he hesitated at first, then when he finally did take her hand, he held it for a long time in his own, without daring to raise it to his lips. But when he finally kissed her fingers and looked up at her his face was calm.

'Goodbye,' he said softly.

And he left.

6

'You'll never get old,' said Carmen Gonzales as she massaged Gladys's long, lovely thighs, 'because you started looking after yourself when you were still beautiful.'

But that wasn't enough for Gladys: she wanted no part of a kind of beauty that was pathetically vulnerable, threatened by age; she needed the brilliant, arrogant triumph of true youth. When even the most lowly passer-by turned round to look at her, when on those March evenings in Nice where flurries of silvery rain patter down, she heard from beneath the arches the voice of a little flower seller say 'Oh, what a beauty! Oh, you're so beautiful!' she felt a kind of satisfaction that was almost physical, like after making love.

These days she could barely tolerate the presence of Lily Ferrer; she looked at the wrinkles on her friend's face with horror.

'She's only fifty after all,' she thought, 'ten years older than me. Ten years goes so quickly . . .' She banished the thought with horror. 'I want to remain young. I don't want to be like the others. I want people to look at me and say, "That Gladys Eysenach is still beautiful."'

And why would they say even that? Who would ever know her true age? She looked barely thirty. She would look the same for many years to come. Thirty ... that was already too old for her. She remembered London, Beauchamp, when she'd turned twenty. That was what she wished to feel once more. She tried to silence the threatening, mocking voice that rose from deep within her: 'That's all gone. Gone ... You might be beautiful for many years to come, seductive even, but not like in the past. You only experience that exquisite bliss, that triumphant joy, once in life. You have to accept that.'

But then she thought, 'Why? What's changed? Mark has left me. Well, there will be other men.'

Mark had left her. For the first time in her life a man had left her. The icy wind of defeat shot through her soul.

No, no. Someone else would come along. She thought of Claude. He had loved her so much. Perhaps he still loved her? As soon as he set eyes on her, as soon as he saw her face, he would be hers. Love, a man's desire, his trembling hands, his eagerness to do her bidding, his loving, jealous looks: she would never grow tired of such things.

In May, Claude Beauchamp arrived in Nice; Gladys ached to see him with a kind of impatience that made her feel so ashamed that she could hardly admit it.

'I find it amusing, that's all,' she thought. 'It will be amusing to find out if he's still in love with me, if he could fall in love with me again. Poor Claude ...'

Feverishly she began making her face and body beautiful. Beauchamp was coming to have dinner with her, alone, at Sans-Souci. At seven o'clock Gladys was already seated in front of her mirror, putting on her make-up. It was a beautiful spring evening, at dusk; the sky looked like green crystal. She thought back to London, the full roses at Covent Garden, going home at dawn after a ball ... How innocent she was then. She could picture the young girl she used to be: her golden hair, her white dress, the corsage of roses, when she'd said to Teresa, 'You don't understand, Tess. You're different. You go through life calmly, coolly. I want my life to be passionate, a fire that devours everything and then dies out ...'

'I'm even more beautiful now,' she continued thinking. 'I don't want him to see the child I used to be: I want him to fall in love with the woman I am now.'

'I miss my youth,' she murmured.

She shivered, then saw her chambermaid standing in front of her.

'Which dress would Madame like to wear?' she asked.

She looked at her without answering, then sighed and said, 'My pink dress and my pearls.'

She had the jewellery brought to her: she wanted to look different from the young girl Claude had desired, as womanly as possible, at the peak of her beauty, dazzling. She followed her chambermaid into her dressing room, the room that Marie-Thérèse called 'Madame Bluebeard's closet'. She took hold of the light bulb that hung from a long cord and walked round the wardrobe. Her fur coats gave off a slight smell of camphor. She felt terribly sad.

'No,' she said suddenly, 'any dress, as long as it's white.'

Finally, Beauchamp arrived. He had hardly changed. Only his hair had gone white. They dined alone on the terrace. Sans-Souci was as artificial as a stage set, but at night it became graceful, elegant, almost rustic. The yew trees that lined the long path, trimmed into the shape of musical instruments, had been obscured by the darkness for a while now. They could hear frogs croaking and a slight smell of hay wafted through the air, mixing with the scent of roses.

'Is it true that you are going back to live in Vevey?' she asked.

'Yes, and I hope never to have to leave there again.'

'Never?' Gladys asked.

'Does that surprise you, Gladys?'

'Yes. Now that poor Tess is dead and Olivier lives in Paris . . .'

'I like it there very much.'

She smiled. 'You're a strange man, Claude. You are my cousin and my closest relative and yet I don't know you any better than a stranger I might pass in the street. Do you really want to spend the rest of your life in that little isolated village, alone, all alone?

'Alone,' she said again, with muffled horror. 'How terrible.'

'Are you afraid of being alone, Gladys? You haven't changed,' he said, looking at her strangely.

'Why should I have changed? Women don't change.'

He said nothing. She was sitting opposite him; she lowered her head; she played slowly, gracefully, with the pearl necklace she wore round her white, delicate neck. She was still beautiful, vulnerable, anxious, touching, but a pale shadow, the ghost of the woman he had once loved. He had seen her several times in the past few years. As for her, she had never once even glanced at him. Every time they saw each other he found her preoccupied with new clothes and new lovers, sparing never a moment's thought for him. Today, however, she was definitely different, eager to please, but as for him . . . Love that is kept secret for so long, locked away in the heart for so long, becomes bitter with age; it corrodes and turns to acrimonious resentment.

'I'm free,' he thought. 'I'm finally free. I don't love her any more.'

'I'd love to see Marie-Thérèse,' he said.

'She'll come and say goodnight to us.'

'How old is she now?'

'Oh! Don't ask me her age, Claude. All I can say is that I try to forget how old she is,' she murmured.

Her hands were shaking. She noticed and pressed them together hard, cruelly, for a long time.

'Are you and she close?'

'Yes, of course,' said Gladys, making an effort to smile. 'She is delightful to me, poor darling. She faces the madness of youth with all the seriousness, all the wisdom of logic and experience! You can't imagine how she treats me. Before every ball I have to go and show her how I look, and if you only knew how harshly she criticises me over my choice of dress or jewellery . . .'

'She's a mother to you,' Beauchamp said coldly.

Gladys slowly shrugged her beautiful shoulders: 'You're making fun of me. But it's true that there's something maternal in the way she idolises me. Because she does love me to distraction. She says the most wonderful things. One day, I can't remember why any more, she said something that brought tears to my eyes: "My poor, dear Mama, you don't understand life . . ."'

'Yes,' said Beauchamp, 'that is amusing.'

Once more, they fell silent.

'I'm happy to see you again,' she said finally, with a sigh. 'What about you? In the past, you seemed to want to avoid me. Why?'

'You're such a woman, Gladys.'

'What do you mean?'

'You're never happy with guessing. You need to know.'

'It's been twenty years,' she said, smiling, 'and I've never asked anything.'

'You'll be disappointed, Gladys,' he said quietly. 'You want me to tell you that I was mad about you. And that's true. But are you asking if I'm still in love with you? No. That's the past. What can I say? Nothing lasts for ever.'

'Is that really true, Claude?' she said, smiling, but a sharp pain shot through her heart.

'You're still beautiful, Gladys, but when I look at you, I don't know who you are any more. To me, you're merely the ghost of what you once were. I'm finally free, happy, set free at last. I don't love you any more. I once loved a young girl in a ball gown who stood on a balcony in London one June evening . . . She mocked me cruelly that night.'

'Just a little, but you're getting your revenge now, Claude.'

'Not really.'

'Just a little . . .'

They looked at each other in silence. She cupped her face in her hand.

'You're holding a grudge against me, Claude. Would it please you to know that you've played a greater, more important role in my life than you could know? I was never in love with you, yet I'll never forget you. I was an innocent child. You were the one who made me realise my power for the first time. You hold it against me, but without realising it, you're the one who poisoned my life. I've never again experienced that feeling of intoxicating pride, never. I never again felt that exact sense of exhilaration. I'm the one who should be holding a terrible grudge against you.'

'Are you mocking me?' he said with a start.

'Now, now,' she said sweetly, trembling with cruel, manipulative emotion. 'All that is in the past. Tell me, you wanted to kiss me back then, didn't you? And you were too cowardly to do it? Well, do it now, and then everything can be forgiven and forgotten.'

'No,' he said, shaking his head. 'As wonderful as your kiss might be, it will never be as sweet as the kiss I desired for such a long time.'

They stared at each other, like two enemies, then Gladys slowly looked away. She let out an angry, stifled, little painful laugh. 'You wanted to see Marie-Thérèse?'

'Yes, please.'

She rang the bell and asked for her daughter. She sat still and silent until Marie-Thérèse came into the room. Her face looked calm but every now and then her mouth grew slightly tense.

Marie-Thérèse and Beauchamp talked, and she answered when one of them spoke to her, but her voice, soft and low, echoed in her ears as if it belonged to a stranger.

'I'm suffering,' she thought, 'but I don't want to, I don't know how to suffer . . .'

7

Beauchamp left. Gladys listened as the sound of the car faded in the distance, then she went out on to the little yellow patio where the lights had just been put out. The night was warm and smelled of the sea and wild mignonettes. Gladys sat down and gently leaned her forehead against the warm stone.

Marie-Thérèse had followed her. They said nothing. Finally, Marie-Thérèse asked, 'Can I put a light on?'

Gladys tilted her head back. 'No, no . . . Go to bed, darling. Go on. I'm tired.'

'Oh, Mama. Do let me stay. I hardly ever see you.'

'I know,' said Gladys. 'You have a really terrible mother, my poor darling; I'm frivolous and I neglect you. But just wait a little while longer. I'll soon be old and hideous to everyone. But you, you'll be beautiful,' she whispered. Her voice had changed. 'It will be your turn to dance and have fun, while I, I'll sit by the fire and wait for you, and I'll have no other pleasure apart from waiting for you, admiring you, asking, "Did you have a good time, my darling?" Or, since I will have become a gloomy old woman, I might even say, "How can you enjoy dancing so much? How can you be so in love with love? How can you love life?"'

A harsh, weary little laugh broke through her soft voice. 'Oh! Marie-Thérèse, promise me that the day you see I'm old, really old, you'll kill me in my sleep.'

She took Marie-Thérèse's hand and leaned her forehead against it, swaying gently. 'That's what I need,' she thought, 'someone to rock me, someone to reassure me. If only I could be like Lily and be satisfied with loving someone. I know very well that I'm still young enough to be in love, but that's not what I want: I want to be loved, to feel delicate, fragile, held tightly in someone's arms . . .'

'Do you love me, Marie-Thérèse?' she asked without thinking.

'Yes, Mama. You shouldn't be afraid of getting old. You're too young, as far as I'm concerned. I feel like I might be able to talk to you better if you had white hair and wrinkles . . .'

'Please, just stop talking,' said Gladys, closing her eyes. 'I don't want to listen. I want to forget, to sleep. Oh, I wish I were a young girl like you with no worries, no problems.'

Marie-Thérèse smiled and gently stroked Gladys's hair. 'You're the one who's the young girl, Mama,' she said, 'and I'm the woman. I've often told you that, but you don't believe me. I know you better than you know me. Are you sure you're my mother? When I was little, I didn't believe it. Perhaps it's better that way? We could almost be sisters, friends . . . we could talk about love.'

'Love?' Gladys said slowly.

'Yes. You must have been loved so much, Mama . . .'

Gladys suddenly stood up. 'It's cold. Let's go inside.'

'Cold? There's not a breath of wind . . .'

'I'm cold,' said Gladys, holding her bare arms close to her body and shivering. 'And don't you stay out here either; go to bed. You're in a cotton dress. You'll catch cold.'

'No I won't.'

'Go to bed. It's late.'

'I'm not tired,' said Marie-Thérèse.

They both went into Gladys's bedroom. Gladys switched on the lights on either side of the heart-shaped mirror. The light was soft and pink. She studied her face closely. Her daughter stood behind her and looked at her mother's reflection in the mirror; she alone, no doubt, saw the first signs of weariness and bitter ageing on her mother's soft face whose features still had the elegance of youth.

'Why is she looking at me like that?' Gladys thought, annoyed. 'Why is she following me around like this?'

'Mama,' Marie-Thérèse said suddenly, 'I need to talk to you.'

'Oh? Well, go ahead, darling.'

'I'm engaged, Mama,' said Marie-Thérèse, looking at her mother.

'Oh, yes?' Gladys said quietly.

She was taking off her make-up. Her long fingers moved slowly and gracefully across her forehead and temples; they started shaking, then stopped at the corner of her large eyes. She leaned forward and looked into the mirror in despair, as if it suddenly reflected the face of a stranger.

'The beautiful Gladys Eysenach,' she mused, 'the beautiful Gladys Eysenach's daughter is getting married . . .'

A sharp, almost physical pain shot through her chest. She continued looking in the mirror and said not a word, her lips clamped shut. She was still beautiful. It wouldn't stop her being beautiful and desirable. She quickly shook her head. No. It might be all right for other women, but no . . . The kind of beauty that was pathetically vulnerable, threatened by age might be all right for Nathalie Esslenko, for Mimi, for Laure, but not for her. She needed youth, absolute success, not a shadow of doubt. 'I can't resign myself to it,' she thought. 'It's not my fault. I don't know how.' But a sarcastic voice from deep within her heart seemed to be saying, 'You'll learn how to step aside, to let your daughter come first; she'll shine at every social gathering and blot out her mother. Men will look lovingly at her, at her young face . . . Soon, some young man will talk about Gladys Eysenach and say, "My mother-in-law . . ." One day, very soon, you will be saying, "My grandchildren." Oh! No, no, it isn't possible. God would not be so cruel!'

'Now that isn't true, Marie-Thérèse, is it?' she said, her voice low and trembling. 'That just isn't possible, now is it?'

'Why not, Mama? On the contrary, it's completely natural. Have you forgotten how old I am? I'm eighteen. I'm a woman.'

Gladys shivered; a look of rage and almost madness shot across her face. 'Be quiet!' she shouted. 'It isn't true! Don't say that! You're still a child!'

'No, Mama, I'm not a child. Do you think that just

because you tell your friends I'm fifteen you can stop time? I'm not fifteen. And you're not thirty. I'm not a child. You always said it and I let you, mainly because I didn't care and, more importantly,' she said, lowering her voice, 'because I was embarrassed for you, Mama, I was embarrassed and felt sorry for you.'

She was standing close, her legs pressed against her mother's knees, and she could feel them shaking beneath her dress. Gladys was hunched over; Marie-Thérèse put her hand on her mother's soft shoulder.

'Poor Mama. Did you really think that all you had to do was make me wear my hair down and no one would ever notice I was a woman?'

'Who is he?' whispered Gladys.

'Olivier Beauchamp, Mama. You really didn't know?'

'No,' said Gladys. 'No, it isn't possible. You're still a child. You can't get married yet. You're teasing me, aren't you? Look at me. Look at your thin arms, your long hair, your little face. You're too young; it isn't possible. You've known Olivier since you were a child; you think you love him but you don't. How could you know what love is when you haven't even known life? Just wait a little . . .'

'I do love him, Mama,' said Marie-Thérèse harshly. 'You must be able to understand that, at least. You must know what love is, don't you? Or do you only see it on the faces of your friends, those old women? I'm the one who's the right age for love, Mama, me, not them!'

'Be quiet!' shouted Gladys, sounding frightened and in pain. 'I will not have it, do you understand, I will not have it! I said you must wait: it is too soon. You will obey me. You will wait. Not now, not now,' she said over and over again, turning pale. She kissed Marie-Thérèse's hands. 'All right? You'll wait until you're more experienced, wiser. You know nothing, you've seen nothing of life yet. Just wait. In two or three years, if you still love Olivier, well, then, you'll marry him. But not now, good God, not now,' she murmured, and she held her daughter close to her, looked at her, beseeching her. She was so accustomed to having her own way that she couldn't even imagine being refused anything. 'You love me, don't you, darling? You don't want to hurt me, do you? And it does hurt me to hear you talk about love, to see you as a woman, already. It's so natural, if you only knew . . . Oh, why are you a woman? If I'd had a son, he would have loved me more. You only think about yourself.'

'But you only think about yourself as well! Look at the kind of life I have. Do you think that books and music and a pretty garden are enough for someone my age? I've had nothing else. You go out and enjoy yourself, go dancing, come home at dawn, but I should be enjoying all those things, Mama, me, even more than you!'

'I never noticed you were growing up.'

'Well, the damage is done now. I'm eighteen.'

Gladys slowly wrung her hands. 'Yes, yes, I know, but . . .'

She could almost hear the other women, her rivals, sniggering: 'Gladys Eysenach? She still looks pretty good. But she's not young any more, you know. Her daughter just got married. Her lover left her. What can you do?

93

She's still beautiful, but ... She's still fairly young, but
...'

And perhaps one day soon they would say, 'Do you
really think she's beautiful? But she's old, you know. She's
a grandmother.'

'Me?' she thought, slowly stroking her face. 'No, no, I
must be dreaming. I was still a child myself only yesterday.
I haven't changed. Only yesterday I was a happy young
girl, a domineering young woman. But Marie-Thérèse said,
"You must have been loved so much ..." And soon
everyone will be saying, "How beautiful she must have
been once ..." No, no, it's too soon. Two or three years
more. That's all I'm asking. That's all I want. For her, it's
so little, but for me ... In three years I'll be old. My
age will be written all over my face. I will resign myself
to it then, like the others. I'll think back to this night
wistfully ...'

'Mama,' whispered Marie-Thérèse, 'answer me. What
about me? You're not listening to me.'

'What do you want me to say? I've already said what
I want. You must wait. What harm would it do you to
wait? You're so young ... To you, the years are light and
sweet; to you ... In three years you'll be twenty-one. You
can do what you please then.'

'I won't obey you,' said Marie-Thérèse, raising her pale,
tense face.

'You have to obey me. And you know it. You're a child.
You're a minor. You have to obey me.'

'But why? Why wait?'

'Because you're too young,' Gladys said again, quietly,
automatically, 'and because these hasty marriages turn

out badly. I don't want you to be unhappy. Yes, I know; you're thinking right now that I'm the cause of your unhappiness. But it isn't true. All I'm asking is a few months of a secret, delightful engagement that will light up your life and give you happy memories. You're still a child, Marie-Thérèse, you don't understand. There is only one thing that makes life worth living and that is the beginning of love, love that is timid at first, that then becomes desire, impatience, anticipation . . . I'm offering you all that and you're holding it against me. I don't want to make you unhappy,' she said again, looking at her daughter in despair. 'Oh, heaven forbid! If you and that young boy love each other, well, then, get married, be happy. I'll be delighted to see you happy. I love you, Marie-Thérèse. But wait a little. Three years will go by quickly and you know very well that I have to consent. But while you wait, take pity on me. Don't tell me anything. I don't want to think about it. I don't want to, I don't want to,' she whispered, hiding her face in her hands. 'It hurts so much. I want a little peace, a little happiness. Try to understand me. Be my friend . . .'

'I don't want to be your friend! You're my mother! If you won't give me your support, your help, your affection, then I don't need you,' Marie-Thérèse said quietly.

'Oh! Marie-Thérèse, how cruel you are!'

'Then give your consent, Mama. You know very well I'll be happy! You're stealing three years of happiness from me, that's all there is to it.'

'No, no, no,' Gladys said weakly.

She was crying; slow, heavy tears flowed down her

cheeks. 'Let me be!' she begged. 'Have pity on me! Don't say anything else. Don't you realise it's pointless?'

'Yes,' said Marie-Thérèse, in spite of herself.

Gladys was holding her hands. Marie-Thérèse pulled away in disgust, pushed away the beautiful, soft white arms that tried to hold her back and ran out.

8

The very next day Olivier asked to see Gladys, but it was the same scenario at Sans-Souci as it had been at the Esslenkos' house: he could only see Gladys with her friends present. That same evening he went to the Middletons' home, where Gladys was invited to dinner.

When he got there the meal was over; a few couples were dancing to the music of a small orchestra. He saw Gladys waltz past in the arms of Georges Canning, Lily Ferrer's lover. She was smiling and looked happy. When she saw him she looked startled and turned pale. He waited until the dance ended, then went up to her and asked to speak to her in private. She was fiddling with a long white glove she held in her hand, gently tapping it against her skirt.

'A word in private? My dear Olivier, can't you come and see me at my house whenever you want? Why so formal?'

'Because it is actually with regard to a rather formal matter,' he said, smiling.

'This is hardly the appropriate time or place . . .'

'In that case, I am begging you to tell me when I can see you.'

She hesitated, then sighed. 'All right, come with me.'

He followed her into a small adjoining sitting room. They were alone. She looked at his face; he looked so like Claude that she felt almost as if no time had passed at all. Like Claude, he had a long, delicate face, fair hair and a slim mouth that looked harsh and severe when closed, but very sweet when slightly open. She smiled shyly at him; he kept his eyes fixed on her, yet didn't seem actually to see her.

'I know that Marie-Thérèse spoke to you yesterday,' he said, 'and you told her you would agree to our marriage under certain conditions. We must wait . . . We must wait three years?'

'That's right,' she murmured.

'But why, Madame? You have known me for such a long time. My mother was your first cousin. You know everything about me. Everything a mother needs to know. You know my family, how wealthy I am, my state of health. Why impose such a delay, such humiliation?'

'I don't see anything humiliating about it,' she said, lowering her head. 'A long engagement is considered natural and very wise in many countries.'

'If the engagement is official . . .'

She shuddered. 'No, not now, no, not right away. Official – that's ridiculous. All the congratulations, the visits, all the hideous bourgeois trappings, no, no, how horrible. Once it has been decided, you will get married straight away and then it will all be public . . .'

'I love Marie-Thérèse.'

'Marie-Thérèse is still a child and so are you. This is a childish whim . . .'

'We love each other as a man and a woman,' said Olivier quietly. 'She is a woman, even though you may never have noticed it. And I'm not just talking about her age: she is courageous, affectionate and loyal the way a woman is. Let us take our chance to be happy. Life is so short . . .'

She started, upset. 'That's certainly true . . .'

'Three years . . . Think about it: isn't it terrible to miss three years of happiness, three years of life?'

'You must learn how to deserve happiness,' she said flippantly. 'Be patient. Believe me, you'll only love each other more. I imagine this isn't the official way to reply to a request of marriage. I never thought it would be necessary this soon; I wasn't expecting it. Good Lord, Marie-Thérèse is still just a little girl to me. How can you not understand that? Until now, I'm the only one she's ever loved . . .'

He quickly shook his head. 'No. Marie-Thérèse is a woman like any other, thank God. When she was a child, she loved you, of course. She had, and still has, great affection for you. But you know very well that the love of a child is nothing when true love comes along. You must have had the same experience yourself . . . like all men and women. So you shouldn't be surprised that Marie-Thérèse loves me more, chooses me; if you continue to oppose our marriage, she will end up considering you an enemy.'

'Oh, no!' murmured Gladys. 'That isn't possible . . .'

Two distinct feelings tore at her heart: she couldn't bear the idea of being hated by Marie-Thérèse, the way she had hated her own mother. But what upset her even more was the thought that, for the first time in her life, she was standing face to face with a man who saw her only as his fiancée's mother, the person standing in the way of his happiness.

'I'm not a woman any more,' she thought. 'I'm just Marie-Thérèse's mother. Me, me . . . Oh, I know very well that it happens to everyone. But death also happens to everyone and who thinks of death without horror? I love Marie-Thérèse, I do, with all my heart; I want her to be happy. But what about me? Me? Who will take pity on me? Of course I think I'm still young and beautiful, but I'm already old to other people, an old woman who will soon be laughed at. "She used to be beautiful," they will all soon be saying. "So many men used to be in love with her." And this young man . . .'

She would have liked him to find her attractive. Not so she could steal him from her daughter. The very idea that Marie-Thérèse might know the desire she felt filled her with shame. She just wanted to see herself in a better light, wanted to obliterate the cruel feeling of humiliation that filled her heart, the pain of wounded pride. She would have loved to make him desire her, even for just a moment . . .

'I only want him to look at me once with desire, no, not even that, just admiration, the way a man looks at a woman; I want him to feel flustered, not know what to say, to fantasise, like so many men before him, and then I'll give in, I'll let him have my daughter, I'll agree to everything, just so long as I know and feel that I'm still a woman. Otherwise, what's the point of living?'

Olivier was thinking, 'They're all alike, these old women. They haven't much time left to enjoy life. So they take it out on us. They may not even be aware of it, but deep down inside they're thinking, "I have so little time left to be happy. Well then, as long as it's within my power, I'll steal a few years of happiness from my children." They tell themselves they are caring, prudent, wise, experienced. In reality they're just plain jealous. They don't want to share life with their children. They curse life, but they intend to hang on to it for themselves, for themselves and no one else. Poor naïve souls,' he mused with pity. He slowly unfolded his long arms, felt the wonderful power of his muscles, the fire in his blood beneath his skin. He remembered how old she was and, suddenly, felt invincible. He looked at Gladys and smiled.

'You know, Madame, three years will pass very quickly, and it will be just as hard as it is now . . .'

Gladys slowly brought her hand to her brow. 'What am I doing? How could I even think of trying to seduce this young man whom Marie-Thérèse loves? How shameful . . .'

'Go now, Olivier, I'm begging you,' she murmured. 'Listen, all I'm asking for is a few months, a few weeks . . . no time at all,' she begged him in despair. 'You must grant me that. I promise you, I swear to you that I'll be good,' she said, like a frantic child. 'Yes. I'll be a good old woman. Just give me one year. What do you say, one year? It's not a lot. One year's grace!' she whispered. 'Wait for one year. You'll have your whole life to be happy, but what about me?'

'You won't prevent me from seeing Marie-Thérèse?'

'No, of course not.'

'You won't take her to the other end of the earth? I'm rather suspicious, you know,' he said, forcing a laugh.

She shook her head. 'No, no.'

'Very well then,' he murmured with a sigh. 'Agreed!'

She stood up, walked to the doorway and gestured to Lily Ferrer as she passed by.

'I want him to go!' she thought, 'I just want him to leave me alone . . .'

Lily Ferrer came over, briskly fanning herself. She was wearing a yellow dress and feathers in her hair; her face was a painted mask.

Olivier exchanged a few words with the two women and left.

'He's in love with you, darling,' said Lily Ferrer, watching him walk away.

'No, he's not,' said Gladys, shaking her head. 'No one is in love with me any more, no one . . .'

She fell silent, holding back the tears with difficulty.

She kissed Lily. 'I'm very fond of you, my dear . . .'

She walked out of the sitting room, crossed the reception room and went out on to the terrace. George Canning was watching her.

'Maybe him?' she thought in desperation.

She smiled at him. He lowered his head and she recognised the furtive expression of an impatient man who is intrigued by a woman, a man who thinks he's the one who has chosen, that he's the one who will win her over.

They walked together down into the garden . . .

9

At the beginning of the war Gladys and her daughter were in Paris, and the Beauchamps in Switzerland. Before leaving for the front, Olivier managed to get to Paris to see Marie-Thérèse. Winter came and Gladys returned to Antibes.

Never had the weather been so beautiful, the roses so sweet. Sans-Souci was deserted, the men servants away at war, the cars and horses requisitioned. Every day Gladys said with a sigh, 'We have to leave . . . What are we doing here?'

But she stayed on because of George Canning. She was having an affair with him; he was handsome and she liked him. She had forgotten Mark, forgotten Beauchamp, forgotten in the way only women can: with difficulty, but completely. She had even forgotten Olivier, it seemed. At the beginning of the war Marie-Thérèse had spoken to her again about getting married, but Gladys refused to discuss it. She had quickly left Paris for Deauville and by the time she returned Olivier was already at the front. She barely noticed Marie-Thérèse. She spoke to her sweetly, as she had always done, using terms of endearment, but she looked through her without actually seeing her, thinking only of Canning, herself and her own happiness. She loved her daughter; she had always loved her, but in the thoughtless, erratic way she loved everything. Her fickle affection was interspersed with long periods of indifference. She was grateful to her for no longer mentioning Olivier's name, for not destroying the complex web of delusions without which she would not know how to go on living.

Nevertheless, it was only in her eyes that Marie-Thérèse could still pass for a child. Marie-Thérèse had changed since autumn: she had become more mature, more womanly, slimmer, and the way she moved was softer and less rushed; her young face had lost its look of innocence and boldness; her body was softer and paler; she wore her beautiful hair tied up.

In October Gladys received a letter from Beauchamp telling her that Olivier was dead, killed at the front. Gladys was alone that night. She sat on the little terrace for a long time, holding the letter. It was a calm evening with not a breath of wind. Finally she got up with a sigh and went and knocked on her daughter's door. Marie-Thérèse was in bed. Gladys walked over to her and gently stroked her hair.

'Darling,' she said, 'are you asleep? I saw you switch off the light as I was coming in.'

'I'm not asleep,' said Marie-Thérèse.

She had pulled herself up on to her elbow and leaned against the pillow; she looked anxiously at her mother, pushing back the dishevelled hair that fell over her forehead.

'Darling, my darling little girl, I have terribly sad news for you and I know you'll feel so much pain that you'll think it will never end, that you'll never forget, but it will pass, my darling, you'll see, it will pass. Poor dear Olivier is dead.'

Without a word, without a tear, Marie-Thérèse grabbed the letter her mother held out to her, read it, then hid her hands beneath the sheet; she wrung her hands so violently that blood rushed to her fingernails. But she didn't say a word; it seemed to take every ounce of her strength to hold back the words that tried desperately to escape her lips.

'My darling,' Gladys whispered with pity, 'I can't bear to see you looking so sad. But it will pass. I swear to you that it will pass. A woman's first love, you know, seems so strong, but it's forgotten so quickly. I know you think I don't understand, that I don't know, that I've forgotten such feelings, but I remember them as if it were yesterday, if you only knew . . . You loved him, I know. But there will be others, Marie-Thérèse. Love is not just a few kisses, a few meetings and lovely plans for the future. You'll only know what love truly is later on, when you're a woman, when it is too late, perhaps,' she said with a strange little passionate but weary sigh. 'You see, I sensed something would happen,' she murmured sincerely. 'I'm so happy now that I didn't give in to your tears, your pleading. A little love affair can be forgotten. But a husband . . .'

'Please, Mama,' said Marie-Thérèse quietly, 'please go away and let me be alone.'

'I can't, my darling, that would make me feel so sad. Don't pull away like that. Cry. Listen to me. You will forget, Marie-Thérèse. You trusted me in the past. I swear to you that one day you'll forget, do you understand?'

She wanted to hold Marie-Thérèse's pale, silent face close to hers; she lightly kissed her.

'Look at me . . .'

Marie-Thérèse looked up slowly. 'I was Olivier's mistress, Mama,' she said. 'I'm pregnant.'

'What?' whispered Gladys.

She leaned forward and looked at her daughter's face: with her plaits half undone, her slim neck and childlike features, she still looked so young that Gladys thought, 'She's lying! It isn't possible . . .'

With a sudden movement she lifted Marie-Thérèse's nightdress over her chest; her breasts were heavy and the colour of white marble that is a sign of early pregnancy.

'You poor child,' Gladys said softly, 'you have caused your own unhappiness.'

'No,' said Marie-Thérèse, shaking her head. 'You're the one who has caused my unhappiness, you and you alone. Why wouldn't you let me marry Olivier? We were young, we loved each other, we could have been happy. Why did you do that? Why?'

'I didn't stop you from doing anything,' cried Gladys angrily. 'You have no right to say that to me! I asked you to wait. You were both so young!'

'And we did wait,' said Marie-Thérèse in despair, 'we waited until death came and took him from me. We waited like good little foolish children, so that you, *you* could be happy, find love, feel passion, while we had to be satisfied with a few kisses, a few lovely plans for the future, as you put it! Oh, I can't forgive myself. You were quite right to say that the young are foolish. Yes, foolish, cowardly

106

and weak, weak when in your hands. What else could we do but wait? When the war started I begged you to let me marry Olivier. You wouldn't even listen. You told me it wasn't possible to allow a marriage with a boy who might soon be killed . . . that your duty as a mother forbade it! Ah, how pleased you were finally to have maternal duty on your side! My goodness, how sincere you were. That was when we realised we'd been duped, realised we had to seize at least a few moments of love, a little happiness. I was the one who wanted to, me,' she said, finally letting the tears flow down her cheeks. 'Poor dear Olivier, he took pity on me. He sensed he would never come back. And so did I,' she whispered. 'I kissed him but in my heart I could hear a voice saying, "He'll never come back." It was a voice I tried to block out, but couldn't. So I begged him to take me, so that for one night I could sleep in his arms and be his wife, and I begged him to give me a child, because I thought, "God will want him to come back if we have a child." But he's dead . . . he's dead . . . It's all over for me now . . .'

'When did you sleep with him?' asked Gladys, grabbing Marie-Thérèse's burning hot hands. 'You haven't seen him since last May!'

'That's what you wanted to believe. You thought I would obey you as I always have, did you? Before leaving for the front he came to Paris. He took a room at the Ritz, on the same floor as us, and I spent one night with him. At least we've had that,' she said more quietly, remembering that night – so brief – the blue curtains, the early dawn light on the bed and that unforgettable sensation of rushing down into an abyss, eyes wide open . . .

107

'But what are you going to do now?' said Gladys, her voice shaking. 'You're not going to keep the child, are you?'

'What are you saying!'

'Marie-Thérèse, don't you know ... Don't you know that you can prevent it from being born, if you want to? It's only two months, it's still possible, quite easy, in fact. You do understand that you cannot keep this child? Just think of the scandal. If people found out ... But you understand that yourself, don't you? Answer me; talk to me; say something. You're not a child any more, sadly, you're a woman, you knew what you were risking, you wanted this. Well, now you have to be brave. You must get rid of the child, all right? You must, Marie-Thérèse! Listen to me, I know a woman ... Carmen Gonzales ... She sells make-up but she's also a masseuse and a midwife, and I know that ... she's done this more than once. It's nothing, Marie-Thérèse, nothing at all. Do you remember my friend Clara Mackay? Her husband was away and she was expecting a baby and she just couldn't have it. She went to see Carmen, in the maternity hospital where she works, near here, in Beix. The next evening she came back and no one ever knew anything. Not ever. Her husband would have killed her. For you, there will be a few moments of pain and then it will be over, this nightmare will end. Say something,' she said, nervously grabbing hold of her bare, slim shoulders. 'You have to do this for the child, for the child as much as for yourself. You can't keep it, let it be born. You don't have the right to inflict life on a child who will be poor, abandoned, unhappy and alone!'

'Do you actually believe I would abandon my child?'

Marie-Thérèse said quietly. 'Quite apart from the unspeakable crime you are suggesting, which is basically the same as smothering him with a pillow the way pregnant servants do. Do you really believe that I'd be ashamed of him, that I'd hide? How little you know me.'

'You're mad,' shouted Gladys. 'You think you're a woman? You . . . You're nothing but an ignorant child. How could you, you, a rich girl from a respected family, want to keep this child? Do you really think I'd allow you to raise this child? Because, in the end, I have some say in this you know.'

'You have no say in it. You shouldn't have prevented us from getting married!'

'And you shouldn't have been that boy's mistress!'

'I'll put up with the consequences, Mama.'

'You're forgetting that you're only nineteen, my girl. For the next two years I have absolute power over you and your future.'

'Well, then, what will you do? You can't kill him.'

Gladys pressed her hands to her face; they were shaking. 'One day, you'll fall in love with another man. You're not going to spend your whole life mourning a lover you spent one night with, are you? What will you do then? Who will marry you with an illegitimate child? Marie-Thérèse, it's not maternal love speaking in you. It's too early for that. You just want revenge. You know that the idea of seeing you a mother, a woman, and doing it this way, hideously, shamefully, is unbearable to me, and that it is to punish me for having made you wait to get married that you are determined to make me suffer. Because you are making me suffer! You'll see that later.'

'Perhaps,' said Marie-Thérèse, lowering her head, 'but I'm not thinking of myself. Does it seem odd to you that it's possible not to think about yourself? Does it? I want my child to live and be happy, and as for me, I'm not afraid of anything, I'll put up with everything . . .'

'You think you will. But you'll see later on . . .'

'Do you think I'll become like you? Well, never, never. You talk to me so sweetly, but you only ever think of yourself . . . and that people might say that you, Gladys Eysenach, are old enough to have grandchildren, to be a grandmother. That's really what you can't bear! You can't even hear the word without shuddering.'

She looked at Gladys.

'You will walk over to your mirror, look at your beautiful face, your blonde hair, and then you will remember that you're a grandmother and life will no longer seem worthwhile. I know you, oh, I know you so well. If I had married Olivier and had a child with my husband, it would have caused you the same unbearable suffering. Only then you wouldn't have dared say a word. But now there's nothing to hold you back. And to avoid becoming a grandmother you're prepared to murder my child.'

'He isn't alive yet,' said Gladys quietly. 'He isn't suffering and that type of crime is committed every day . . .'

'Well, it's not going to happen to me,' said Marie-Thérèse, sounding almost wild, thinking that the child she was defending this way, and who existed only to her, was more precious that anything else in the world.

Gladys started pleading again. 'All right then, it's what you want; he's yours and you have the right . . . But don't you owe anything to me? To yourself? To me,' she said again in despair. 'Can you imagine the scandal . . .'

'Yes, I can,' said Marie-Thérèse, smiling slightly.

'So you don't have any pity for me?' said Gladys hopelessly. 'What have I ever done to you? It isn't my fault . . . Could I possibly have foreseen the war? It happens every day that parents oppose a marriage that isn't suitable. What else have I done?'

'Other parents mistakenly believe they're doing the best thing. Their children might suffer, but they don't have the right to hold their mistakes against them. But you, you thought only about yourself. You didn't want to have a married daughter. You didn't want to be "the mother of the young Madame Beauchamp",' she murmured, sobbing hoarsely. 'You wanted to snatch away a part of my life, my share of happiness, the way you always have.'

'That isn't true,' said Gladys. 'I've always loved you.'

'Yes, when I was a child, when I was a good excuse to make people think well of you,' said Marie-Thérèse bitterly. 'You sat me on your knee and let people admire you. And I, idiot that I was, loved you so much; I admired you so much; I thought you were so beautiful! I used to talk to you as if you were the child, I, your daughter, as if you were my child. Now I hate you; I hate your blonde hair and your face that looks younger than mine. What right do you have to be beautiful, happy and loved, while I . . .'

'That's not my fault . . .'

'Yes it is,' shouted Marie-Thérèse. 'You should have been thinking of me and only me, the way that I think only of him,' she said, wrapping her weak arms round her body. 'Leave me alone! Go away; get out!'

'You will not keep this child, Marie-Thérèse. He'll live, he'll be well looked after, I'll give him all the money he needs, but you will not keep him, not that . . . you won't show him off. That's impossible. Oh, I can tell very well what you want, you know. You want me to suffer, don't you? If I ever hear you say the word "grandmother", I'll want to kill myself,' she said quietly. 'I'm in pain! You can't understand that. You think I'm a monster. But I'm right, I am, because I see life as it truly is, so short, so sad without love, without men desiring you, with its long, horrible old age! But you, you're young. You'll forget your Olivier. I wasn't asking for an eternity, you know! Just two or three more years. But no, you'd fix things so that everyone would know the truth, so that at every moment I'd be expecting someone to look at me oddly or whisper with pity, "Is it possible? She seems so young, but . . ." And what about all the women? The way other women, my enemies, my friends would laugh at me? Just wait a while, wait two or three years and you'll see, you'll see, I'll be a good mother, you'll have nothing to complain about, and as for the child, well, perhaps I'll even love him then. So tell me you won't keep this child?'

'I *will* keep him, I *will* know him, I *will* bring him up,' Marie-Thérèse said harshly. 'Now get out.'

She threw herself back on to the bed and lay there without moving, without a word, without a tear. Gladys kept talking to her for a long time, but she bit into the sheets and remained silent. Finally, Gladys left.

10

Gladys forced herself to accept that the child would be born; she resigned herself to it but life had a bitter taste. Whenever she saw a man smile as a pretty young woman passed by, she felt her heart being ripped apart. Sometimes, the man would look at her first, but that had no effect on her, she was used to that. What she couldn't bear was that he looked away, looked at someone else . . .

One evening, at Lily's house, she met a woman who was blonde, like her, and whose fragile, triumphant beauty was similar to hers, but she was young . . . she was young . . . Gladys smiled at her, spoke to her, but the woman's flawless skin, her youthful eyes were a living insult to her. For weeks she avoided going back to Lily's, so as not to see her rival again.

Sometimes she would leave Nice, but she carried within her a kind of repressed anguish that would wake her up in the middle of the night. She would get out of bed, take off her nightdress and walk naked over to the mirror. She would study her face, her body and, for just a moment, she would feel calmer. She knew very well that she was beautiful. It was dawn, the time of day when the last fires were put out in the hotel fireplaces, when some stranger sighed and dreamed in the next room. She would slowly stroke the light wrinkles that insomnia had drawn across her brow, but which would be gone in an hour. That was nothing, meant nothing. It was something every woman worried about. It had nothing to do with the mysterious pain she was feeling, the shameful jealousy that filled her heart with venom.

'I mustn't think of myself. I must forget about myself,' she thought. 'There's Marie-Thérèse. Her poor child . . . The war . . . And here I am, a weak, miserable creature who is thinking about my beauty, my youth. But I want to be wiser, I want to be better . . .'

George Canning had joined the army and been at the front since January. Everything was changing all around her. Everything was cold and sad. At Sans-Souci there were no more parties, not a soul. She had kept on only her chambermaid and a young lad from the village to replace the gardeners who had left. Marie-Thérèse rested in her bedroom or in the garden, by herself, all day long. In the evening they sat opposite each other, each of them thinking about the child. Sometimes Gladys, as if suddenly awakening from a dream, would see her daughter's face and notice how thin it was, how worn out with waiting for the child to come. Then she would look at her with pity. She was worried that she was so pale, so sad.

'Come on, now, eat something; you'll never be able to bear it if you don't eat, if you don't build up your strength. What can you do? It's a terrible thing, but you must be brave, darling. You're so young. Everything passes, is forgotten. Olivier . . .'

'I'm not thinking about Olivier, Mama. You don't understand. I'll think about Olivier after the child is born. Now, all I want is to see that the child, that his life . . .'

'The child . . . the child . . . If you didn't have this child you could have the most wonderful life; you could forget, get married, be happy . . .'

'But I am having the child, Mama.'

'Yes, you are,' whispered Gladys with hatred.

When the birth was near, Marie-Thérèse would go to Carmen Gonzales, who would deliver the baby. Carmen was worldly and nothing shocked her. She would take the child, keep it and look after it, do as she was told.

'Why are you worried?' she asked Gladys. 'You're rich, aren't you? You have money? Well, with money, life is all roses. Come on, now, come on, you're not the first person this has happened to.'

'Mama,' said Marie-Thérèse one evening, 'I don't want to go to that woman's house. I find her repugnant, and she frightens me. I want to go to a hospital, in Paris or Marseilles, anywhere, but not to her.'

'She's the only one I trust to be absolutely discreet,' said Gladys.

'The whole world can know, as far as I'm concerned; why should that matter to me?'

'I know! You've said that already, more than once, shouted it out. But I don't want anyone to know. Do you hear me? I'm begging you, begging you, stop talking about this child, let me forget. What difference would that make to you? Why talk about it before he's even born?'

But Marie-Thérèse loved this child that did not yet exist with passionate tenderness, this child to whom she alone gave reality, a face, a name . . . With each passing day she grew heavier and more tired. She could only walk with difficulty now, only just managed to get out of the house. She despaired at how weak she felt. Her mother would never let her keep this child, never. She was only nineteen. She had nothing that belonged only to her. For two more years she would be at the mercy of this woman who was blinded by her own desires, who cared about nothing but herself and the fact that she would soon be getting old. Sometimes she wanted to talk to her, to beg her not to abandon the child if she herself were to die, but she couldn't bring herself to say the words. She saw the way her mother looked at her pregnancy and turned away in hatred. The child . . . How vividly she felt him alive within her. She slowly stroked her body and felt as if she could feel him tremble, moving beneath her fingers. She imagined her child's body, voice, eyes, his smile. She dreamed about him. She knew what colour eyes he would have. Every so often she forgot Olivier. Olivier was dead. He was now no more than a partially decomposed corpse dressed in rags, in no man's land. She could do nothing for him. But the child, the child had to live. She wrapped her arms round her warm, pulsating womb where the child lived, moved. She was afraid of Gladys, afraid of Carmen . . . especially of Carmen, afraid of her fat little hands, her voice, the muffled sound of her felt shoes . . .

'They'll take him away from me,' she thought, 'while I'm too weak to fight for him. He'll be badly looked after, badly fed, poor and alone, all alone . . . my baby, my child . . .'

She remembered a story she had heard in the past, she

couldn't remember when, or where . . . a vague story she'd heard a servant tell, about a child, born in the middle of the night, on an isolated farm, and whose grandparents had taken him and buried him alive. In the morning, when she woke up, his mother had found him gone.

She clasped her trembling hands tightly together. 'Never, I'll never leave you, my baby . . .'

Baby . . . It was the sweetest word she could think of, the only word . . . She adored him. He had only her and his life depended on her alone. At night she talked to him softly, reassuring him, saying, 'There now, don't be afraid of anything. We'll be happy . . .'

When she realised the child would soon be born she thought, 'I won't call for anyone. I'll wait until the child is either born or I die. And once he's born, no one in the world will be strong enough to take him away from me. I'll hold on to him so tightly, I'll hold him so close to me, so close to my heart, that no one will be able to take him away from me. And if I die, he'll die with me.'

11

Gladys was alone in her room, sitting in front of the fire. Marie-Thérèse lived far away from her, in another wing of the house, separated from hers by an entire floor. She couldn't hear the low groans that her daughter was hiding beneath her blankets.

It was a calm night, without a hint of a breeze; the leaves on the palm trees barely rustled in the wind; the sea, lit up by the moon, was as white and creamy as milk. Cool air wafted up from the tiled floors. The chambermaid had lit a fire in the fireplace and Gladys was absent-mindedly poking at it, tilting her long neck: it was so supple, so soft, so white . . . She couldn't bring herself to go to bed.

'When this is all over,' she thought, 'I'll take Marie-Thérèse away from here and we'll never come back. She'll forget. She's still only a child. It's a terrible thing, but she'll forget. There will just be one more useless little creature in the world. Why didn't she listen to me? How I want this all to be over. What a nightmare . . .'

She stood up, sighed, went out into the garden, slowly walked through the cedar trees, made her way down to the sea, came back up and threw some little stones against Marie-Thérèse's dark windows, quietly calling out her name. Marie-Thérèse was doubtless asleep. Poor child . . . What a sad start to life.

'But she's young,' she thought, with bitter jealousy, 'there's no unhappiness that doesn't fade with time. She knows nothing, understands nothing yet. Ah, I would have gladly traded places with her. None of this matters when you're twenty. I would have accepted all the sadness, all the suffering, if only I could have been young again.'

She went back inside. The house was silent. Her chambermaid had turned down the bed and set out her long lace nightdress. She got undressed and took off her rings. Then she went to sit in front of the fire again, counting the months that had passed since the beginning of the war, since Olivier had gone. The child would soon be born.

'The child . . .'

She couldn't say the words 'my grandson', not even to herself.

'Never,' she thought, 'I'll never let her keep him. Whatever she says, however much she cries, it will make no difference. He will be happy, well cared for, he'll want for nothing, but I'll never see him, never know his name. But even then, just knowing he exists, that he's alive, will be enough to poison my life.'

Her heart was heavy. From now on, to Marie-Thérèse, she would be the enemy and she knew it. That caused her pain. She needed to be loved.

'Well, it's all over now,' she thought, trying to mock herself. 'There's no way around it, I'll be an old woman.

Even if I look young and remain beautiful, in my heart I'll know I'm an old woman. Marie-Thérèse wants to keep her child. Poor innocent girl. What is a child? Someone to take our place, to push us to our death, someone who keeps on saying, "Get going now, go away, it's all mine now. Give up your piece of the cake. You've eaten it? Have you had enough now? Well, then, go away!" That's what a child, even the best child, thinks of us. "Have you had enough now?" But it's never enough, never.'

She felt an overpowering wish to die.

'That would be the best thing, and in her hard, virtuous heart, Marie-Thérèse might think, "This is my punishment." Does she really have a hard heart? She used to love me. But is it my fault that Olivier died? Could I have foreseen the war? But it's not Olivier she won't forgive me, it's the child. Never to see her child, never to hear his cry!' she whispered.

She moved closer to the fire, heard the chambermaid walking in the next room and called her in.

'Did you light a fire in Mademoiselle's room, Jeanne?'

'Yes, Madame,' Jeanne replied.

'Did you see her? Did she need anything?'

'I knocked on her door, about an hour ago,' said Jeanne, coming into the room. 'She said everything was fine and that she was about to go to bed.'

They looked at each other and sighed.

'This is so terrible,' said Gladys, looking away, 'you know, my poor Jeanne, so terrible . . .'

'As long as no one finds out,' said Jeanne quietly, 'and Mademoiselle has her mother. How many girls are all alone when the same thing happens and they have to hide from the very people who are the only ones who could help them. It's a great blessing to have your mother with you.'

'I can't forgive her,' said Gladys with difficulty.

'I know, but that's understandable, it brings dishonour,' said Jeanne, shaking her head. 'But, Madame, you must take pity on her.'

Jeanne had been in the service of the Eysenachs for several years. She was a woman of forty, with a full, tanned face and small, dark, lively eyes. Her hair was beginning to go grey. She had had the simplest of lives; she had always been a chambermaid. She knew nothing apart from her profession, could barely read and write, just knew how to mend lace, iron the clothes and get passionately involved in the lives of her masters. She enjoyed debts that needed to be hidden, love letters she had to deliver. She was never as happy as when there was a sick person to tend, a child less loved than the others to take care of, a woman neglected by her husband. When it came to the love life of her employers, she had an extraordinary gift of clairvoyance that was almost prophetic, the kind that only servants or children possess. Gladys had not even attempted to hide Marie-Thérèse's pregnancy from her: she knew only too well it would be utterly pointless; but she knew also that Jeanne would say nothing, that Jeanne felt keenly the shame of this illegitimate birth: she had the utmost regard for bourgeois respectability. Thanks to her, no one knew about Marie-Thérèse's condition: Jeanne herself had requested that the other servants be sent away: no one came into the house; no one saw Marie-Thérèse.

'No one has any idea, Madame,' she said again.

Gladys didn't reply. Jeanne picked up the clothes that Gladys had thrown on to the floor and left.

Gladys looked at her bed and sighed. She would have liked to drown her sorrows, go dancing and drinking, but it was wartime. Nice was as austere and gloomy as the rest of France. All her friends had gone. All her lively, frivolous little social circle had fled. All the villas were shut up.

'The day will come when the war will be over, and everything will be delightful and happy, the way it used to be, and I . . . Oh, how am I to bear it? How can I live with the knowledge that one day I'll be old? Everyone knows they're going to die. But it's funny, I'm not afraid of death. I would be afraid if I believed that death wouldn't be the end of everything. But I know very well that it is the end.'

She recalled Richard's pale face as he slept in her arms; he looked so peaceful . . .

'He wasn't afraid of death either, but he wouldn't have been able to put up with destitution. He wouldn't have been able to stand being poor or losing his power. Well, for me, for a woman, it's the same thing, exactly the same thing. I want a life that's worth living, otherwise, what's the point of living at all? What will life have to offer when I'm no longer attractive? What will become of me? I'll be an old woman plastered in make-up. I'll pay for lovers. Oh, it's horrible, horrible! I'd rather throw a stone round my neck and sink to the bottom of the ocean. Can anyone see in my face that I'm going to be a grandmother?'

Tears were streaming down her cheeks. Angrily she wiped them away with the back of her hand.

'There's nothing I can do, nothing . . .'

She shuddered and watched the flames rising in the fireplace. It was so quiet. Only the sound of croaking frogs filled the night. The sea was shimmering. What was Marie-Thérèse doing?

'Does she really deserve to be pitied? That's life, after all . . . One day she'll probably regret having suffered in the past. One day, when she's loved and happy. Will she be happier than me?'

She smoked one cigarette after the other, watching the ash burn down, then throwing them into the fireplace. She shivered and crossed her arms inside her wide sleeves.

'I never used to feel the cold. Now I'm frozen to the bone whenever a breeze comes in through an open window.'

She couldn't get to sleep. She could hear her heart beating. She wanted to remember the balls, her conquests, the parties. Ah, was there anything more wonderful in the world . . . ?

She would make her entrance and everything around her became . . . not exactly silent . . . but attentive. Everyone who looked at her confirmed her beauty, her power. So many men had been in love with her . . .

'That was all I ever cared about,' she thought. 'All I ever really loved was their desire, their submission, their madness, my power and pleasure. But so many women are like me. Do they all suffer the way I do, women who aren't stoic mothers or from the boring middle classes? Yes, of course, of course. It's horrible to have equated pleasure with the meaning of life only to see pleasure flee beyond your grasp, but what else is there in this world? I'm just a helpless woman . . .'

She stretched out her hands towards the fire, then stood up. The piano lid was open. She played a few notes. Yes, there was music, poetry, books . . . but she knew very well that those things were only useful to be more seductive, because even the most beautiful face can look tired, unattractive in a moment of boredom or fatigue; but to her, as for most women, such things meant nothing, they didn't really affect her. A few passionate, melancholy lines of poetry, some beautiful lyrical words: they were just offerings to a man, for him alone, and when the man was gone, nothing remained.

'At least I'm honest,' she murmured with a little laugh; she was surprised to hear the sound echo in the silent room and it made her shiver.

She walked slowly towards the bed, got in and fell asleep.

She dreamed that Marie-Thérèse was dead. She dreamed she was locked in a dark, shadowy room and that Marie-Thérèse was stretched out on the bed, dead. She knew she was dead. Yet the pale young woman in the bed was speaking, seeing and could hear; she looked like a fading picture of the real Marie-Thérèse, like her reflection. Marie-Thérèse was lying on her side and she was smiling sweetly, affectionately. Gladys could see the pure outline of her pale, hollow cheeks. Marie-Thérèse raised her hands. She heard Marie-Thérèse's voice saying, 'How I love you, my darling Mama. I've never loved anyone but you.' She pointed to a small child's bed: it was empty. And in her dream, Gladys leaned forward in anguish and, seeing that the child wasn't there, she thought, 'I knew very well that it wasn't true, that it was impossible, that there was no child.' She felt extraordinary relief rush through her, a kind of heavenly joy that made her whole being glow. 'Where is the child?' she asked. But Marie-Thérèse smiled sweetly and replied, 'There is no child. Whom do you mean? You are my child.' She touched Marie-Thérèse's forehead and asked, 'Are you going to get better, my darling? I love you so much . . .' How she loved her at that moment. 'No,' replied Marie-Thérèse. 'Can't you see that I'm dead? But it's better this way. Everything is better this way.'

She woke up to the sound of Jeanne's voice near her bed. 'Madame, come quickly! You must come quickly! It's Mademoiselle . . .'

'Has she had the child? Is he alive?'

She felt fierce anguish, fierce hope.

'Oh, Madame, you must come right now, right now!'

Marie-Thérèse was in her room, stretched out on the blood-soaked sheets. She was holding her child tightly against her lifeless breast.

'She didn't call, Madame,' said Jeanne. 'She had her child all alone, the poor thing. She must have died of a haemorrhage. I heard a cry and I came in. But she wasn't crying, it was the child. She died without calling for help, alone, all alone.'

Slowly Gladys walked towards the motionless face. How different it was from her dream. It had an expression of hatred, fear and terrifying courage. Marie-Thérèse clutched her miserable child in her stiff arms with all her strength; he was covered with blood and panting, but life coursed through his entire body.

12

Gladys went back into her room an hour later. It was finally dawn. She paced back and forth through the room for a long time, then threw herself on to the bed and closed her eyes. But she immediately heard the sharp, weak little whine of the child, whom Jeanne had put to bed in the next room.

'Marie-Thérèse is dead!' she groaned out loud.

And it was only when she actually said the words that the tears welled up in her eyes.

She went back to see Marie-Thérèse. Jeanne had cleaned everything up. Marie-Thérèse was stretched out on the bed; her little face looked like wax and her head was thrown back, deep into a pillow; her hands were crossed at her waist. Gladys was shaking; she put a fur blanket over her daughter's cold feet: she couldn't bear the idea of those frozen feet. For a second she forgot that the child existed; he had stopped crying. Marie-Thérèse's features had lost their weary, tragic expression; she now looked grim and cold. Gladys slowly stroked her hair.

'My little one,' she said, sobbing deeply.

Every now and again her sadness would subside; all she felt was a kind of stupor; she wanted to make herself suffer; she forced herself to conjure up certain images, memories, but they made her feel such sharp despair that she grew afraid.

When Carmen Gonzales arrived, she rushed towards her and grabbed her hands. 'She's dead, did you see her?' she murmured, 'She's dead . . .'

'Did she kill herself?' Carmen asked in her dry voice.

'Kill herself? Oh, my God, no. My poor little girl. Why would she kill herself? No, it was an accident, it was surely a haemorrhage. She didn't call for anyone. Why, why didn't she call for anyone?'

'Listen,' said Carmen, 'there's no point in crying now. The real bad luck was when the poor girl . . . But now, perhaps everything has happened for the best.'

Gladys started. 'What?' she said.

'You have to face the facts. What would have happened to her? Who would have ever married her? Someone after her dowry, some crook. And as for you, if people had found out . . .'

Gladys wasn't listening. 'It's not my fault,' she thought in despair. 'She never heard a single word of reproach from me. I would have done anything for her.'

'What is it?' asked Carmen. 'You look like death. Go to bed and let us take care of everything,' she added, looking at Jeanne.

'What do you have to do, my God?' murmured Gladys, hiding her face in her hands. 'I've already told you, she's dead . . . dead . . . There's nothing to be done.'

Carmen shrugged her shoulders. 'Well, if you really want the whole world to know . . . Come on, now, go to bed, don't worry about anything.'

She forced her to get into bed and rubbed Gladys's cold feet to warm them. 'You're frozen . . .'

That word, that gesture, reminded Gladys of her dead daughter.

'Oh, Marie-Thérèse, my little Marie-Thérèse,' she groaned and her sobbing was so loud, so violent, that its suddenness and intensity surprised Carmen.

'Marie-Thérèse . . . Marie-Thérèse . . . Her poor little cold feet, her frozen hands . . .'

She cried for a long time, then lay motionless, her eyes staring and sad.

Carmen sat down next to her and patted her hands. 'There, there, try to think straight. What can you do? None of this will bring her back, will it? It can't be undone, of course, but . . . Tell me, what about the child? The baby?'

'The baby?' Gladys repeated quietly.

'Yes. You don't want to keep it, do you?'

'No, no,' murmured Gladys, speaking with difficulty. 'I couldn't. Don't ask me to do that. It's impossible . . .'

'Listen to me. Let me tell you what I honestly think. It will be your decision, naturally. Believe me, you mustn't do things by halves. Keep him with you, raise him, if you like. But if you don't want to keep this child and give him your name, it would be better for both of you if you gave him up right away. It would be best to hand him over to an orphanage and be done with it. And of course, you could always get him back later on, if you change your mind. But if you think you can have someone raise him far away from you, hide from him, and count on the fact that no one will know anything about it, that you might go and see him from time to time without anyone being the wiser, well, that's nonsense. That would be leaving yourself open to blackmail. Do you understand?'

'No,' said Gladys, 'no, not that, not an orphanage ... Have him raised far away ... Make sure no one knows ... I'll pay whatever it costs.'

'With money, anything is possible,' said Carmen, sighing. 'If you wish, we can find someone to raise him far from here.'

'Yes.'

'I'll arrange everything. Don't worry. Fortunately, she died a natural death. I know someone in the Mayor's office,' she said, leaning down to whisper in Gladys's ear, 'someone who sometimes does me favours. I'll have the official papers say that the child was born in Beix, at my clinic, and that the mother and father are unknown. The document will go through with the others. That should keep any indiscretions to a minimum. As for your daughter, perhaps you could say she died of a chest complaint, what do you think? That would explain why she hasn't been out for some time. In any case, there isn't a soul in Nice, and there's the war. No one cares about what's happening at his neighbour's place. That's one lucky thing in all this mess. Can Jeanne be trusted?'

'Yes,' whispered Gladys.

'Call her.'

Jeanne came in. Her face was red and her hands were shaking. She held the newborn baby close to her breast.

'No one, apart from you, knows anything, is that right?' asked Carmen. 'If you hold your tongue, Madame will make it worth your while.'

'What are you going to do with the baby?' asked Jeanne.

'I'm going to find someone to raise him. What do you want us to do with him?'

'Would you like to see him?' asked Jeanne, without answering Carmen.

She held the baby out to Gladys.

'No,' Gladys said with difficulty, gritting her teeth, 'I don't want to see him.'

'It's not the child's fault, Madame,' murmured Jeanne.

Suddenly, Gladys felt terribly weary. She shrugged her shoulders and said, 'All right then, give him to me.'

'After all, Madame is his grandmother,' said Jeanne, shaking with anger.

Gladys's pale face turned bright red. A wild, almost mad expression shot across her face.

'Take him away! Take him away! Don't show him to me, I never want to see him, never! I hate him! I'll give him money; I'll give him everything I have, but I never want to see him again!'

'*I'll* keep him, Madame,' cried Jeanne.

Gladys fell back on to the bed, sobbing, clutching on to Carmen's arms. 'Do whatever it takes. Leave me alone! Won't you take pity on me? Do you want me to die? Well, I'd gladly die if that would bring back Marie-Thérèse! Go away and leave me alone! I can't look at him. He means nothing to me! I refuse to accept he shares my blood. He doesn't exist! I don't want to know that he's alive. Take him away.'

As soon as Jeanne and the child had left the house, the savage fury that had grabbed hold of Gladys subsided. She pushed Carmen away, went into her daughter's room and collapsed, sobbing, at the foot of the bed. Her heart was breaking.

'Why did you do it, Marie-Thérèse?' she groaned. 'Why did you leave me? I'm alone, all alone now. Dick is gone, and now you, my little girl, and there's not a soul in the world who loves me any more.'

Carmen brought her some mourning clothes and helped her dress. Gladys was silent and trembling, more beautiful than ever, her eyes burning and dry. Every so often she pressed her hands to her heavy chest and thought, 'If I could cry, it might hurt less . . .'

But not a single tear fell from her eyes; only a harsh, hoarse little sob escaped her lips every now and again.

'It will pass,' said Carmen, staring at Gladys with her piercing, scornful expression. 'Come on, now, it will pass. You're too much of a woman to be a mother for very long. Too young to suffer for long . . .'

'Be quiet,' said Gladys softly.

'Listen, can you give me your documents for the official paperwork?'

'I don't have any of them here.'

'Never mind; it doesn't matter, we'll sort it out. But tell me, how old was the poor girl? Fifteen, am I right?'

'No,' murmured Gladys, 'that's not right. You know very well, Carmen, that she was nineteen.'

'If you take my advice, you'll say she was the age everyone thought she was: fifteen. She looks like a child, stretched out like that with her hair down. No one will think to suspect the truth. It would be better that way for her memory and for you.'

'For me . . .' said Gladys, then said no more.

What difference would it make to Marie-Thérèse?

She handed Carmen a cheque. 'This is for Jeanne, for the child. And she can come and see me later on. The child must want for nothing; I want him to be happy. And later on, who knows? I have no one left in the world . . .'

'Yes, who knows,' said Carmen again and a shrewd, intelligent look flashed across her heavy face. 'You could adopt him one day. You might love him, one day, like a mother. Who knows?'

13

Gladys left for Madrid, where she lived until the end of the war; afterwards she travelled some more; in 1925 she was back in Paris. On New Year's Eve she was dancing in a fashionable nightclub in Montmartre; it was a narrow cellar with red walls. It was nearly dawn; the dancers' faces were taut with fatigue: they danced as if they were very drunk. The music was no more than a muted drum that beat out the rhythm to keep the crowd in time. Some couples weren't dancing any more, just walking slowly, swaying in each other's arms, without thinking, without any desire, their minds a blank.

Gladys was dancing among the others. The first year after her daughter died she had worn white mourning clothes, and she continued wearing them: she looked good in white. She hadn't changed. Her hair was just as blonde, her face as delicate as in the past. Only her cheeks looked more taut and, when she was tired, you could see the outline of her fine bones and deep-set eyes; the shadow of a skeleton appeared beneath the youthful skin. For her skin remained remarkably young and she still had the figure of a young girl, soft and supple.

That morning, under the early morning light that filtered through the folds of the curtains, her fine, pale blonde hair framed her forehead like a halo of luminous smoke, and the only sign of age was the hollow in her cheeks that nothing could hide. Her long white back was bare; as she danced, she tilted her head slightly, lowered her wide eyes and smiled with weary, ravishing elegance at the men who surrounded her.

Sometimes, when by some miracle she saw a young face, a young body among the painted mummies in the nightclub, Marie-Thérèse's face would rise up in her mind. As she danced in the arms of a man, her lover who held her close, she'd think of Marie-Thérèse with tenderness and despair. But Marie-Thérèse was dead. 'She's happier than I am,' she thought. She had blocked out the circumstances of that death the way that women can: by forgetting, innocently and completely. When she pictured Marie-Thérèse in her mind, she saw her as a child, as the child who had loved her. She sighed and looked sadly around her, but the people dancing, the smoke, the empty bottles were the setting of her normal life, and it didn't seem any more inappropriate to think of Marie-Thérèse in such a place as she did when in her bedroom. Yet she pushed away the thought. What was the point, what was the use in regretting the past? She had so little time left to live. She had to push away such black thoughts. She looked up at the man who held her in his arms.

Her obsession had become fierce and desperate: her lovers lasted only a day now, sometimes only an hour. She had to be sure of her power, sure she could drive a man wild, as in the past, sure she could make him suffer. When she could see them suffering her heart would feel appeased, but not for long. It wasn't easy. Since the war, it was rare to find a man who was prepared to suffer over a woman. And she was no longer the most sought-after woman, the one who is noticed first among the herd of other women, the one whose brilliance overshadows all her rivals. She was no longer the woman men looked at immediately. Of course, she still easily aroused love and desire, but men grew tired of her. With each passing year they got bored with her more quickly. She gave in to them easily, for she knew very well that men were now eager for love, but she was too used to being adored to yield to such silent, brutal desire. She needed reassurance that she was loved, needed to hear tender words, needed time and the knowledge that a man was jealous, but every now and again a kind of desperate tempestuousness would evoke a secret distrust of her in the young man with whom she was in love.

'I'm not getting tied down,' they all thought. 'She's beautiful, desirable, but there are so many other women . . .'

Sometimes she would find a man who was young, more naïve than the others, who loved her the way she wanted to be loved, but she would immediately get tired of him. 'No,' she would think, 'he's too easy. But that other man, his friend, who hasn't even given me a second look . . . Oh, my God! Let me have that once more. Once, just once, to be attractive, as I used to be, incredibly and utterly attractive, and then that will be the end; I'll be an old woman, my heart will be dead.'

But she loved the fierce, capricious excitement, the

passion that burned through her body and the wild, bitter, tragic existence of the years that followed the war.

'Ah,' she mused, 'now is the time to be young . . .'

The memory of her youth filled her with envious suffering. She grabbed the hand of the man sitting beside her; she looked into his eyes; she leaned her anxious, trembling face towards him. How men had changed. Richard, Mark, George Canning, Beauchamp . . . and now these bored faces, cold eyes, weary voices and such brief, brutal desire . . .

She went home at dawn. Outside her car the city was coming to life; it was covered in a bluish light; a breeze blew across the Seine; her heart ached; she remembered moments from her youth, the open carriage, her long white gloves, courtly love . . .

'Men have changed? You poor fool. I'm the one who's changed, me . . . Everything disappears? No, but we, we disappear.'

She sighed with ironic sadness. Then she looked into the little dusty mirror and saw a miraculous picture of youth.

'I must be dreaming,' she thought. 'I'm still beautiful and as young as before! Who would ever believe I'm past thirty?'

Of course, in 1925 a woman's age scarcely mattered. Forty was still young.

'How could I have been afraid to turn forty? Ah, I wish I were forty again. At forty, you're at your best, in your prime, still young. Yes, but . . . fifty . . . fifty. That's harder!'

She allowed the man beside her to touch her breasts, but secretly despaired.

'Yes, go on, you can look for more beautiful ones, but you won't find them!'

Of course . . . But if he knew . . . If he realised 'Gladys Eysenach is fifty', what would he think then? What would he say if they quarrelled? If any man ever said 'At your age', she was sure she would die of shame.

'If he loved me,' she thought, 'it would be different. But there's not a soul in the world who loves me.'

She so wished she might hear words of love as in the past. Was that gone for ever? Or rather (and this is what made her despair), were men saying those words to someone else?

She tried to reassure herself: it was the fault of the time she was living in, such brutal casualness, such eager, hurried lovemaking, and immediately afterwards such cold boorishness: 'dropping a woman', turning up at assignations looking bored and tired, setting a heavy price for favours, as women did. And when she asked; 'Do you love me?' the reply: 'How very 1900 of you, my dear . . .'

That generation, however, was getting older. Others replaced them, young boys who were the opposite of their elders: passionate, emotional, bitter. But they seemed to care for her less and less, for it isn't enough to keep your face and body young; you have to speak, feel and think exactly like the twenty-year-old children, but without overdoing it, without appearing old-fashioned, without flattery . . .

She was the mistress of a young Englishman; he was as lovely and youthful as a girl.

'Are you fond of me?' she asked shyly, forgetting that

she had already asked him the same question as he held her in his arms.

'Oh, hang it all, Gladys, a fellow can't jabber all night about love.'

Little by little the depressing anxiety that grew within her led her to frequent brothels. There, at least, desire was genuine. Every time she waited in the Madame's little sitting room, her heart beat rapidly, echoing in her chest, she recalled the intoxication of the past: she was still under its poisonous spell, as if venom flowed through her blood.

Like all obsessions, this one did not give her soul a moment's peace. Just as a miser thinks only of his gold or an ambitious person of attaining honours, so Gladys was in love with the desire to be attractive and with her fear of growing old. 'Nothing would be easier,' she thought, 'than to hide my real age.'

The war had scattered everyone who had known her in the past. And even they . . . Time goes by so quickly . . . Everyone forgets so completely . . . And, for women, contrary to what is believed, there exists a kind of secret pact where age is concerned. 'I won't make fun of you, if, in exchange, you will spare me. I'll flatter you, I'll say I think you're beautiful, but when the occasion presents itself, you'll put in a good word for me, some little compliment that will allow me to feel my proud youth and smile at my lover with less fear and humility. I'll pretend to forget how old you are and you won't remind your circle of friends that I too am past fifty. Have pity on me and I will not be cruel or betray you, my poor sister, my comrade. I'll say, "How ridiculous, you're only as old as you look" and "Have you heard about that famous actress? Her lover is cheating on her? She's keeping him? How do you know? And how many young women are deceived the same way?' Never will I shout, "Let's mock that old woman!" And you, you will do the same . . .'

Gladys would be the first to speak: 'Why talk about how old a woman is?' she'd ask, smiling. 'In this day and age, no one's interested. If a woman is beautiful and seductive, what else matters?'

Before, she used to say nonchalantly, with ease, 'Life is too long. What are we meant to do with so many years?'

Now, a sort of superstitious fear prevented such words from leaving her lips. She never spoke of the past, not about Richard or Marie-Thérèse. She had put away all the photos of Marie-Thérèse that used to hang on the walls of her house, for the style of the dresses that the little girl wore were all too revealing of their time. She had kept only one photo of Marie-Thérèse, when she was seven, half-naked, with her hair falling down over her eyes. 'A little girl whom I lost,' she would say, sighing.

Everyone thought that Marie-Thérèse had died as a child. Even Gladys had ended up believing it.

She travelled constantly. She never expressed concern about burning her bridges behind her, which sometimes made her seem like an adventuress. 'I'm bored of this place,' she would think, but in reality she would leave because she'd seen someone she'd known in the past, or had gone to someone's house that brought back too many painful memories. It was no longer the light-hearted passion that used to drive her from one place to another, but a kind of tragic fleeing from the past.

On the day of her fiftieth birthday she couldn't stop thinking 'You're fifty. You, Gladys, who only yesterday ... You're fifty, fifty, and you'll never be young again.' It was on that day that she went to a brothel for the first time and ever since then, every time her depression became too bitter to bear, every time she was tortured by doubting herself, she would go and spend an hour there.

Whenever some man she'd never met before was more eager, more generous than usual, a sort of heavenly satisfaction filled her heart.

'But what if someone recognised me?' she thought. 'I'm free. And besides, what would they say? That I'm depraved? Ah, they can say I'm depraved, or mad, or a criminal, as long as they don't say I'm old, that I can no longer inspire love, anything but that abomination, that horror!'

When she was sure that she was attractive, that the man was looking at her with admiration, even after lovemaking, she felt a shiver of joy that was almost physical, a thousand times sweeter than the other kind. Here was a man: a businessman with a clean-shaven, cold face. Ten years ago she wouldn't have looked at him twice. Now he was asking, 'Could we meet again somewhere else?'

And she felt overwhelming satisfaction rise up in her heart.

She had reached that age when women no longer change: they simply decompose, but in a way that is hardly noticeable, beneath a mask of powder and make-up. Paris was indulgent, spared her, along with the others. She was graceful and elegant. If someone said, 'Gladys Eysenach?

But she's an old woman . . .' another voice would immediately reply, 'She still looks so attractive. It's so natural, so like a woman to wish to remain young. It does no harm to anyone.'

She kept her delicate bare neck uncovered in the cold wind; in the street, her body was so svelte that she looked like a young woman and her face looked thirty, perhaps forty, though only early in the morning or late at night. But she wasn't satisfied with that: she wanted to be twenty again, to dance until dawn, then to look as smooth and fresh as a flower, without powder or lipstick, as she had in the past.

In the street, a man turns round and smiles at her. She looks at him calmly, indifferently, like a woman who isn't interested. The passer-by is in a hurry; he walks away. And she, who at first had shivered in delight, now anxiously tries to remember: 'Would that have happened with a man in the past? Wouldn't he have kept trying? Wouldn't he have followed me anyway, just for the pleasure of watching my beautiful body from behind, trying to imagine the curve of my hips under my clothing? But what was the point of thinking of the past? The past doesn't exist. These are just dreams, memories of a time gone that weigh down on me and obsess me. Lucky Marie-Thérèse,' she sometimes thought, 'to be taken by death while still so young. Youth . . . The passion of youth . . . All passion is tragic, in the end; every cursed desire is tragic, for you never really get what you dreamed of.'

Depressing thoughts at early daybreak after staying up and drinking all night, thoughts that taste of ashes, bitterness and absinthe: New Year's Eve always made her feel like this.

At the next table a woman smiled at Gladys. She had dyed hair and her pendant fell between her hideous, grotesque, sagging breasts. Though her eyes – her old, sunken eyes did try to smile, the rest of her face was so scarred, plastered over, stitched together, that a smile couldn't easily spread across its painted surface.

'Gladys . . .'

Drunk, stiff, carefully holding a glass of champagne in her hand – it was covered with rings and deformed by gout – the spectre walked towards Gladys. 'You don't recognise me. Oh, my darling, what a joy it is to see you again, truly a joy! And still so beautiful! You haven't changed at all, really. It's Lily Ferrer. Ah, how I resented you. Do you remember George Canning? He was so handsome! He was killed in the war. So many dead,' she cawed, 'so many dead.'

She sat down next to Gladys. She looked at her affectionately: it did her good to see a woman, barely ten years younger than herself, who retained such miraculous youthfulness. A wonderful gift, even if granted to someone else, raises hope within the heart. 'It could happen to me. Why not? Yes, in spite of the reflection I see in the mirror, in spite of the young lover I pay, why not?'

'And who's the lucky man, Gladys? I've had terrible disappointments, great sadness, yes, I have. A young man in whom I had placed all my trust betrayed me horribly. But that's always the way it's been. I've never had any luck,' she said, sighing. 'Are you happy?'

Gladys said nothing.

'No? Ah, men have changed. Do you remember? In our day,' she said, lowering her voice, 'such manners, such devotion. Men would love a woman for years without even a word of encouragement. They would give up everything for her. Lose everything for her. And now? Why is it different? Why? Is it because of the war?'

Gladys stood up and held out her hand. 'Forgive me, darling. My friend is calling to me. Goodbye. It was nice to see you again. But I'm leaving tomorrow, leaving Paris . . .'

Suddenly Lily remembered something. 'Your daughter must be grown up by now. Is she married?'

'No, no,' said Gladys hastily, for her lover was coming towards her. 'No. Didn't you know? She died . . .'

'How terrible for you,' murmured the old woman compassionately.

She kissed Gladys on the cheek with her painted lips; it left a smudge of lipstick that Gladys tried secretly to wipe away from her trembling face.

'You poor, poor darling. You loved her so much . . .'

Gladys walked over to join her lover who was standing at the door. He had heard Lily's last few words.

'You had a daughter?' he asked as he followed her through the crushed streamers and confetti that slid away beneath her high heels. 'You never told me. Was she still a child when it happened?'

'Yes,' said Gladys in hushed tones, 'a very young child.'

It was raining. The street sloped down towards the place Blanche, shimmering and flickering in the early dawn light.

14

In the spring of 1930 Gladys met Aldo Monti. He was handsome. He had a square, hard, clean-shaven face, a heavy, masculine head and piercing eyes. His features bore an almost inhuman expression of determination and self-control, the kind you no longer find on English faces, but only on foreigners who are trying to copy them. All his life, Monti had forced himself to appear English in his speech and mannerisms. He was even careful of his thoughts, out of fear that they might not be pure enough, English enough. He did not possess a great fortune. He skilfully managed his money, but life was starting to become difficult.

Very quickly, he pictured Gladys as a possible wife. She was beautiful. She was extremely rich, and her money was from honourable sources. He found her attractive. Certainly, she had had other lovers, he knew that, but her affairs had never been sordid or self-seeking. He courted her for several months, cunningly and cautiously, then asked her to marry him.

They were visiting some Italian friends of Monti who lived in Paris. It was a beautiful autumn day and the garden was still full of sunlight. At the entrance of the house, you could see a shaft of light, as soft and golden as honey, through which shone the women's light dresses.

Gladys wore a muslin dress and a light, almost transparent straw hat that half covered her lovely hair. Beneath the short white little veil, her wide, anxious eyes rarely looked directly at anyone, and even then she would quickly lower her eyelids. She walked slowly next to Monti until they reached a bronze fountain whose edges were carved with a cluster of naked children. She leaned against it and, without thinking, began stroking the beautiful, cold, polished little bodies.

'Gladys, my darling, please be my wife. I don't have much to offer you, I know. I'm poor, but I have one of the oldest, most respected names in Italy and I would be so proud to make it yours. You love me, don't you, Gladys?'

She sighed. Yes, she did love him. For the first time in many, many years, she saw in a man something more than an affair with no future. Here finally was someone who was offering to be with her for eternity, to reassure her, to protect her from herself. She was deeply weary of the pursuit of love that had become her life. Anxiously counting her conquests that became more precarious and difficult, seeing lonely old age edging closer and closer with each passing day. What a nightmare! Finally, she would be sheltered away from life on a warm, strong man's shoulder, not someone passing through her life for a moment, but another Richard; she'd found another Richard. She lowered her eyes. He looked at her fine lips; she was wearing lipstick; her mouth looked anxious, tense at the corners. She didn't reply.

'We'd be so happy together. Please marry me,' he said again.

'It would be foolish,' she said weakly.

'But why?'

She said nothing. Marriage ... Her date of birth ... He was thirty-five and she ... She couldn't admit her exact age even to herself. Mad, painful shame swept through her. No, never, never! Even if he married her in spite of that, how would she rid herself of the idea that he only wanted her money, that he would leave her one day, perhaps not soon, or in a year, but in ten years. Ten years would go by so quickly. And then ... He'd still be young, but she ... 'But actually, God is granting me a reprieve,' she thought desperately. 'One day, if I'm ill or have a fever or am tired, I'll wake up and I'll be old, old, old ... And he'll know ...'

'No, no,' she said sweetly, 'not marriage. Can't we go on loving each other with no obligations, no ties of any kind?'

'If you loved me,' he said coldly, 'you would find such ties pleasant and easy. If I mean anything to you, Gladys, you must marry me.'

Then she thought it might be possible: with money, and running the risk of a scandal and blackmail, she could change her identity documents to hide the date that haunted her thoughts, her sleep, her dreams. She was a woman; she had never looked further than tomorrow.

'You mean more to me than you could ever imagine, my darling,' she said to Monti, with her dazzling, weary smile.

Their engagement was made official and a little while

afterwards Gladys left to go back to the country where she'd been born. There, she got a copy of her birth certificate, scratched out a number from the date and, with this fake document, she saw to it that all the other documents she'd ever been given throughout her life were corrected. When she got all the revised papers back, she returned to the little village where she'd been born and found some official pen-pusher who was willing to change her birth certificate to the same date as the other documents. It cost her a fortune, but in the spring of 1931 she finally managed officially to take ten years off her age. Just ten years, because far away there was a child's marble tombstone with a false date, and that date was impossible to change.

Ten years. She could admit to being forty-six, ten years older than Monti. Her age, her sin, her crime still haunted her. To this man whom she loved, she wanted to be a child, weak and delicate once more, held tightly in his strong arms. She had to be understanding, maternal, but she wanted to be loved and admired, the favourite among all women, not as a friend, not as a wife, but as a mistress, as the radiant young woman she once had been in the past.

She never found the courage to marry Monti.

15

One autumn day five years later, Gladys was on her way home; she was walking down an empty road that ran alongside a wood. It was getting dark, even though it was barely four o'clock. Dusk in Paris had the scent of a damp forest. Gladys had sent the car and driver away; she walked quickly, enjoying the smell of the fresh, humid air. There was not a soul in sight. Only a dog ran on ahead of her, sniffing the ground. The houses were dark behind their closed shutters; the empty little gardens glistened, moist from the rain.

Suddenly she saw a young man standing beneath a lamppost; he was wearing a grey raincoat but no hat and he seemed to be waiting for her. She looked at him in surprise and automatically reached up to touch her pearls beneath her fur jacket. He let her pass, but when she was a few steps ahead of him he began to follow her. She walked more quickly, but he soon caught up with her; she could hear him breathing behind her. She walked faster. Then he stopped, seemed to disappear into the fog, but a moment later, after she'd forgotten about him, she could hear his footsteps behind her once more. He followed her in silence until they reached a lamppost and then called out to her quietly, 'Madame . . .'

He had a thin young face; his long, delicate neck tilted forward, as if it were being pulled by the weight of his heavy head.

'Won't you listen to what I have to say, Madame? Are you afraid? I'm not a thief. Look at me.'

'What do you want?'

He didn't reply, just continued walking behind her, so close to her that she could hear the sound of his breathing. Then he began whistling *The Merry Widow*, endlessly repeating the first few bars. She listened with strange anxiety to his whistling and the rhythmic, halting sound of his footsteps in the empty street.

She stopped and opened her handbag.

The young man gestured her to stop. 'No, Madame . . .'

'Well, then, what is it that you want?'

'To follow you,' he said in a low, passionate voice. 'It isn't the first time. You won't be angry with me, will you, Madame? It's not the first time this has happened to you, is it? A man hiding in the shadows, following you? In despair? You've never noticed me? Yet I've been watching you in the street for a month now. I see you leave your house and come home late at night. I see your friends. I see you get into your car. You can't imagine how all that makes me feel. But until now I've never managed to find you alone. You won't be angry with me, will you, Madame?'

Gladys looked at him and shrugged her shoulders slightly. 'How old are you?'

'Twenty.'

'And you're following a woman you don't even know?

Why waste your time like this?' murmured Gladys. Her demon, the desire to be seductive took hold of her and, without meaning to, her voice grew softer.

'You seem like a good person, Madame. Would you happily be charitable and grant a look, a smile, at a young man who thinks only of you? Oh, and for such a long time now,' he said, his voice strange, trembling as if in a passionate dream.

'You're just a boy,' said Gladys. 'Look, be reasonable. I've listened to you patiently, but you do understand, don't you, that you must leave me alone. I have a husband,' she said, smiling. 'He might not take this childishness very well.'

'You don't have a husband, Madame. You are perfectly free and alone. Oh, so alone . . .'

'In any case,' said Gladys nervously, 'I am asking you to go away.'

He hesitated, bowed and leaned back against a wall. She saw him fiddling with his long red scarf. She walked more quickly, looking for a car, but the street was deserted. After a few moments she heard the young man's footsteps echoing behind her once again.

This time she stopped and waited for him. When he caught up with her, she said angrily, 'Look! That's enough now. You are going to leave me alone or I will make a complaint to the first policeman I see.'

'No!' said the young man harshly.

'You're mad!'

'Don't you want to know my name?'

'Your name? You are mad!' she said again. 'I don't know you and I am not interested in knowing your name.'

'That's not exactly right. You don't know me, it's true, but you will be extremely interested in me once you know my name.'

He paused for a moment, then said once more, very quietly, 'Extremely interested.'

Gladys said nothing, but he could see the corners of her mouth tremble and droop.

'My name is Bernard Martin,' he said finally.

She let out a strange little sigh, like a stifled sob.

'Were you expecting a different name?' he asked. 'I have no other names.'

'I don't know who you are.'

'Yet I'm your grandson,' said Bernard Martin.

'No,' she stammered. 'I don't know you. I don't have any grandchildren.'

She was almost sincere; she couldn't manage to link the memory of a nameless child, that little red creature she'd seen twenty years before, with the sight of this young man standing in front of her in the rain. Twenty years . . . Time would never pass as slowly for her as it did for other people.

'Come on, now, Grandmother, you'll have to accept it; I really am your grandson and, believe me, it wouldn't be difficult to prove it: I have a letter from Jeanne, your old chambermaid, who brought me up. She died, but her letter is very moving. I have my rights . . .'

'Your rights? I owe you nothing!'

'Ah? Well, then, I'll lose my lawsuit. But what about the scandal? Can you imagine the scandal, Grandmother?'

'Don't call me that!' cried Gladys, starting in blind fury.

The young man didn't reply. He put his hands in his pockets and started whistling *The Merry Widow* again.

151

Gladys dug her nails into her hands to control the trembling that shook her whole body. 'Is it money you want? Yes, I . . . I have been neglectful. How could I have forgotten you for such a long time, my God? I told Jeanne to contact me as soon as the money ran out. She never did, and I . . . I forgot,' she said quietly.

'I never wanted for anything. It's not money that I'm after.'

His disgusted tone of voice dispelled any remorse and pity she might have felt.

'It's the scandal, then? Of course. My poor boy. You must come from some godforsaken hole in the country. The scandal, as you call it, in Paris . . .'

He said nothing and continued walking alongside her, whistling in a low, thoughtful way.

'He's Marie-Thérèse's son,' she thought.

But that idea aroused no emotion within her heart: it was completely filled with the dull echo of fear.

'Is it money you want?' she asked again in despair.

The young man spoke with difficulty. 'Yes.'

She quickly opened her handbag, pulled out a thousand-franc note and put it in his hand.

The boy shook his head and said, 'Your lover is called Aldo Monti, is he not?'

'Do you think you're frightening me? Exactly why do you think my lover would care if my daughter once had a child?'

'That's true, Grandmother, that's true. But I've spoken to Carmen Gonzales, you see, and Jeanne who brought me up. Those two women know you as only servants can know their masters; not a single bit of your heart was

152

unknown to them. You didn't abandon me because I was an illegitimate child, but because you didn't want anyone to know how old you really were. I detest you.'

'Leave me alone!'

'It's true that you still look young. What do people say about you? "She's forty? Fifty?" Have you resigned yourself to being forty-five? A grandson of twenty, after all, isn't so terrible. Perhaps I'm mistaken? Am I? Well, am I? Oh! How I wanted to see you close up, hear you speak! You're just as I imagined you . . . But no, no, even though I'd heard you were still a beautiful woman who looked young, I imagined you as a monster. And you are a monster.'

He leaned in towards her intently. He looked at her blonde hair and her made-up face, and she tried to see in his features something of Marie-Thérèse and Olivier Beauchamp. But all that was in the past. They were dead. There was only one true thing in the world: Aldo, her lover! This thin, delicate boy looked no more like Marie-Thérèse and Olivier than a caricature looks like a charming photograph. He was pale; his heavy mop of hair fell forward over his forehead; he was badly shaven and still had some hair above his lip; his long cheeks were so thin they were almost transparent. Only his eyes resembled Marie-Thérèse's eyes: passionate, clear, with long, dark eyelashes, even more beautiful because they shone in his thin, ugly face.

He spoke first. 'Listen carefully,' he said, sounding cold and threatening. 'If you don't want to spend every night on the telephone, because I'll call you continuously, and if you don't answer, I'll bang on the door of your house so hard that you'll have to open it and let me in, if you don't want any scandal, if you don't want me to write to your lover, then come and see me. I live at 6 rue des Fossés-Saint-Jacques. It's a student house. I'll wait for you every day until six o'clock. Make sure you come.'

'Do you really think I'll come?' she murmured, forcing herself to smile.

'If you're smart you will.'

'Very well. I'll see, I'll . . . Just go now, I'm begging you, just leave me alone! I'm not as reprehensible as you think,' she added, sounding insistent and fearful.

He didn't reply, just shook the rain from his hair, closed the top button of his raincoat and walked away.

16

That night she made Monti stay with her. They dined together in front of the open window. The trees of the Bois were hidden behind a heavy, reddish autumn mist. It was starting to turn cold. Monti stood up to close the window, but she seemed to enjoy the cool air.

'A young woman would feel cold tonight, half naked as I am,' she thought, 'but I : . . .'

She would have braved fire, walked on water, to prove to herself that she was strong, lithe, young . . .

Paris was damp and as mauve as a ploughed field under a murky sky. Beneath the trees the beams of car headlights appeared, grew larger as they passed, then turned into little golden sparks amid the branches.

Monti shivered. 'Really? You aren't cold?'

'No. You're so sensitive to the cold, my darling. Shame on you . . .'

Gladys liked having the window open: that way, the only light came from the Paris sky and a small, shaded lamp at the back of the bedroom. She was afraid of bright light. Monti was smoking. He was nervous; she could sense it; tears welled up in her eyes, adding to her terror.

'Please don't let him speak to me harshly the way he sometimes can,' she thought. 'I couldn't bear it tonight . . .'

She closed her eyes, trying to picture Bernard Martin's face. Suddenly she shuddered.

'What's the matter, Gladys?' Monti asked.

'Nothing. Oh, nothing,' she replied, her voice sounding tearful. 'Come and sit beside me, Aldo. Do you still love me, even a little? Oh, tell me you do, please, please tell me. Men don't like talking about love, I know,' she said, forcing herself to smile. 'My darling, my beloved . . . I love you so much, if only you knew how much. My lips quiver whenever I look at you. I'm in love with you the way a girl of fifteen would be, but you, my love, you feel only lukewarm towards me, as if we were an old married couple. I can tell . . .'

'Gladys, you're the one who feels weary and lukewarm towards me because you refuse to do what I've been asking you to do for so long. Be my wife. I want to live with you; to be with you all the time; I want to take you back to Italy and give you my name. Why do you refuse?'

She shook her head and looked at him in anguish. 'No, no, I asked you never to speak to me of that again. It isn't possible!'

He said nothing. But in spite of what she said, she was thinking that on the contrary, she had never been as tempted to agree, to go away with him, to tell him everything, finally to be relieved of carrying within her the weight of her fear. She had no one else in the world.

For an instant she thought, 'Why not? What difference is there between forty and fifty and sixty, if you're no longer young, no longer truly young? Nothing can replace that.'

She remembered women who were past sixty and were still loved, or so it was said. 'Yes, and they're the ones who say it,' she mused with sad lucidity, 'but in truth, they're only loved by gigolos, or former lovers who still love them only because they remind them of their past. If only Dick were still alive. I would never have been old to him. But Monti . . . To admit to him: "I'm sixty. I have a twenty-year-old grandson . . ." I'd feel so ashamed. I want him to admire me, to be proud of me. I want to be young. I *was* young until now. No one suspected how old I was. And now . . . But what can I do for that boy now? The damage has been done. Giving him money is easy enough. But will he be content with money? He must hate me.'

She hid her face in her hands.

'Darling, what's wrong with you tonight?' asked Monti, surprised.

'I don't know,' she murmured in despair. 'I'm sad. I want to die. Let me sit on your lap. Rock me.'

He held her close; she snuggled up against him, enjoying the wonderful sensation of feeling so small and lithe in his arms. He stroked her hair, calling her 'my little one, my dear little girl . . .' Time no longer existed. Gladys's heart melted with sweet sadness.

'If he knew how old I really am, how could he ever say such words? What would happen if a young man of twenty called me "grandmother" in front of him? But I'm young, I'm young, this is all a horrible dream.'

She wrapped her arms round his neck, breathing in the

delicate scent of his cheeks; his eyes were closed, his fine nostrils dilated.

'I'm too heavy, Aldo. Let me go.'

'You're as light as a bird.'

'Aldo, will you always love me?'

'You don't usually want to talk about the future, do you, darling?'

'That's right, because it's frightening. Listen to me; close your eyes and answer me truthfully. This is extremely important. Will you love me when I'm old?'

'But aren't you forgetting that we shall grow old together? Aren't we about the same age?'

'No,' she said, shaking her head. 'If you only knew how frightened I am of getting old . . .'

'Darling Gladys, you're young and beautiful.'

'No, no, that's a lie. I'm an old woman,' she said in a subdued voice.

'Right now, my darling, you're nothing more than an illogical child.'

'How long can a woman be desirable?' she asked suddenly. 'Until what age?'

'What a question, my darling. As long as she is beautiful and feminine. Fifty, fifty-five . . . That's so far away yet, Gladys. A lifetime . . .'

'Yes, a lifetime,' she whispered.

'By then, we'd be an old married couple, believe me. We'd both have white hair. Is that so terrible if we're together?'

'And love will have disappeared?'

'Of course not. It will be a different kind of love, that's all. You're talking like a child, Gladys.'

'When I was very young,' said Gladys, 'I promised myself that I'd kill myself if I ever felt I was old. I should have.'

She didn't even hear the consoling words he was saying to her. She had closed her eyes and kept her face hidden in Monti's arms.

'Oh, Aldo, I'm so unhappy!' she said, bursting into tears.

'But why, my darling, tell me why so I can help you. Ah! You don't trust me. You don't even consider me your friend.'

She put her arms round him and hugged him with extraordinary strength for a woman who appeared so frail. 'No, no, not a friend! You are my lover, you are everything I love most in the world! Don't listen to me! I've been frustrated by ridiculous things all day, a dress that didn't fit, a bracelet I lost, who knows?'

'You're a spoiled little girl, my darling, too spoiled to be on this earth.'

'You're making fun of me, but . . . I've had my share of unhappiness,' she whispered.

'You never talk to me about that.'

'Good Lord, what's the point? Aldo, I'm not letting you leave tonight.'

He laughed and shrugged his shoulders. 'Whatever you want.'

When he was finally asleep, she got into bed next to him, but she remained awake, unable to close her eyes. Eventually she got out of bed and went quietly into the room next door. She was shivering with the cold now. She paced back and forth in the room, silently. 'No one in the world, no one . . .' She wrung her hands as tears flowed down her cheeks.

'Dick, oh Dick,' she whispered in despair, 'why did you have to die?'

But he'd been dead for so long, buried beneath the ground. She thought of Mark, also dead. And George Canning, killed. There was only one man left: Claude . . . and that young boy, that stranger who was a grandson to both of them.

She found a sheet of paper and began to write, listening out for Monti's breathing in the next room. 'Please come and help me . . . Don't be surprised that I am appealing to you for help . . . I imagine you've forgotten all about me? But I have no one else in the world. Everyone else is dead. I am all alone. Sometimes I feel as if I have been buried alive, in a pit of loneliness. You alone can remember the woman I used to be. I am ashamed, desperately ashamed, but I want to have the courage to ask your help, you and only you, because you once loved me . . .'

'He's forgotten all about me,' she thought in despair. 'He's old now, free, free and living in isolation. *I'm* still burning in hell, but he's calm, he's detached from everything, of course, and he's old, old. How could he understand? Ah, I chose to burn in hell until my very last day; I rejected the peacefulness of old age. But I'll make up for everything; I'll ask that young boy to forgive me. I'll do everything for him, everything that a mother can do for a child she has brought into the world, everything that Marie-Thérèse would have done, just as long as he keeps quiet, just as long as Aldo doesn't find out!'

In the morning she locked the letter in the desk drawer, but she would never send it.

17

The next day the telephone rang every fifteen minutes. Bernard asked for nothing. All he did was hang up when he heard the chambermaid's voice. Finally, Gladys had the telephone brought into her room and, trembling, she answered it. 'It's me, Bernard.'

'Hello!' said the familiar voice. 'Is that you, Grandmother?'

'I gave you a thousand francs yesterday. Can't you leave me in peace for a few days?'

'Did you really think that would settle the score?' said the voice.

'Will you just tell me exactly what you want?'

'Over the phone?'

'No, no,' murmured Gladys; she could hear noises in the next room. 'I'll call you back.'

'No, you'll come and see me.'

'No!'

'As you please. By the way, what's the name of your fiancé, my future grandfather? It's Count Monti, isn't it?'

'Listen to me,' said Gladys in anguish, 'you're playing a dangerous game. This is nothing short of blackmail.'

'And you know very well that it is a very specific kind of blackmail.'

She went to see him. He lived in a stuffy, dark little room with a low, dirty ceiling. A deep crack ran across the marble sink; the bedclothes were worn out and yellowish; a thick lace curtain covered the windows.

'What a horrible room,' murmured Gladys. 'You can leave here whenever you like, my dear boy.'

He looked at her and smiled. 'No, that's not what I need. You don't understand. I can assure you, you don't understand.'

Some books were open on the table, others covered the floor; a plate of oranges sat on the bed.

'Listen,' said Gladys. 'What do you want from me? There's just so much I can do to make amends for the past, but . . .'

She fell silent, expecting him to say something, but he just stared at her.

'Go on, Madame, I'm listening. Would you like to sit down?'

She obeyed mechanically; when she realised that her hands were shaking, she hid them beneath her fur coat.

'Why do you want a scandal?'

'But, Madame, you misunderstand me. You persist in believing that I wish to prove I have rights, and I do not, because I'm illegitimate, I know that. But that's not what this is about. At least, I haven't properly considered that part yet. I simply feel a need that will seem strange to you: the need to make my presence felt in your life, the need to disturb your magnificent peace of mind. Look at yourself in the mirror. At this moment, you don't look like the woman you were yesterday, only yesterday, when you so graciously spoke to the strange young man who was following you in the street. You look your age now, my darling Grandmother. Come now, don't be annoyed. Don't disown me. After all, I'm your flesh and blood. The only reminder left of a daughter whom you adored, judging by the magnificent white marble mausoleum you had placed in the cemetery in Nice. I've seen the grave. I've seen the Gonzales woman. Charming creature. How well I understand that my mother chose to die rather than have that woman at her bedside.'

'Who brought you up? Was it Jeanne?'

'No. She took a job, so she could continue earning her living and supporting me. She entrusted me to her cousin, a former cook who lived with Martial Martin, a retired butler. He was a stupid but honest man who agreed to claim I was his so I could have an official status that was honourable, if not exactly lofty. He died when I was still a child. I was raised by Berthe Souprosse, Jeanne's cousin. Mama Berthe, I called her.'

Gladys hid her face in her hands.

'They told you everything?'

He shrugged his shoulders and didn't reply. In fact, the two women had never forgotten a single detail of what had happened the night he was born; they barely spoke of anything else, nor did they think of anything else, which is what happens when ordinary people witness a tragedy whose protagonists are richer and more powerful than they are. At the beginning they didn't talk about it in front of the child, but he used all his passionate, hungry, patient intelligence to piece together the truth from bits of their conversations, their sighs, the knowing looks the women gave each other. Their memories from the night he was born, Marie-Thérèse's death, Gladys's attitude, her character, to him, all those things took on the curious fascination of a work of art. At night, after they'd put him in the large bed where he slept next to Mama Berthe, they would sit in front of the lit stove in the dining room and knit while tirelessly retelling the same story.

Through the half-open door, the boy could see Berthe hunched over, her triangular black shawl over her shoulders, the long steel hairpin that held up her white hair beneath the fluted frill hat she still wore. Jeanne would mend Bernard's shirts and his velvet short trousers. The child would be half asleep, but even in his dreams he would hear Jeanne telling the story over and over again. Certain phrases were repeated night after night, so Bernard knew them by heart.

'Shameful! There wasn't even a vest to put on the baby in a house that was overflowing with money. His grandmother spent a hundred thousand francs on the grave of that poor mademoiselle, a hundred thousand francs before the war, and that little boy, who is her own flesh and blood, could have died without her giving him a second thought.'

Bernard would rub the sleep from his eyes, wake up and listen closely, and he nurtured a complicated, passionate feeling of hatred in his heart that he fed, allowed to grow, and which brought a bitter yet exquisite sensation to his life.

Now, he contemplated Gladys with cold curiosity.

'What do you want from me?' she asked again, trembling.

'We'll talk about it another time,' he murmured, and

smiled. 'Today, I don't want anything. Today, all I wanted was to see you and to speak to you.'

'I won't be coming back . . .'

'Oh, but you will. There's no doubt about it. You'll come back as soon as I tell you to.'

'No.'

'No?' he repeated mockingly. 'You're thinking that you'll go away now, aren't you? You're thinking, "I'm rich. I could go to the other end of the earth tomorrow, if I wanted to. This miserable little kid won't find me." But a letter would find Count Monti, of course.'

She didn't reply. She tried to find something of Marie-Thérèse in his features. She recognised nothing of her bloodline in him. Bernard's voice was soft and feminine, but his laugh was harsh.

'Old age will be upon me in a few years, a few months perhaps,' she thought to herself, sighing, 'real old age, the kind that is pure peacefulness and renunciation. The day will come when I'm tired of love, and since there are no miracles in this world, since the only person I gave birth to is dead, why not this boy? I would have a home, a place where I could be at ease. Of course, I've been guilty of things, but . . .'

For who has ever looked into his own soul and condemned himself unreservedly?

'I was young, too beautiful, spoiled by my life, by men, by the world, spoiled by love . . .'

She wanted to say it out loud, but Bernard's sharp, pale, ugly face and the spark of intelligence that burned deep in his narrow, bright eyes prevented the words from leaving her lips. She looked once more at his miserable student

165

room, the dirty windows, the worn-out rug and the photo of a woman that sat on the table.

'Who is that? Is she your mistress?'

He didn't reply.

'I didn't come because of your threats, Bernard. Don't think that's the reason. You can't understand. If you were a woman, you'd understand how you could spend a whole part of your life in utter ignorance, how you wouldn't notice time passing, how it's possible to have a man's love in your heart and forget everything else. I haven't come here as your enemy. How could I?'

'But you did think about going away, didn't you?' he said, breaking in.

'Yes, but I know that a letter would get to my lover. Can't you see, I'm not defending myself. I'm not denying anything. All I want is to help you. I'm rich. I can see to it that you have an enviable life.'

'So long as I stay away from you, right?'

She looked at him in anguish. 'What do you mean?'

'So you're happy to give me money, are you? But what if it's something else I want?'

'I am prepared', she said weakly, 'to love you like a mother.'

He let out a dry little laugh. 'Who's asking you for love? Who needs you any more? Young gigolos, no doubt, and that Monti, who must be a pimp?'

'Monti is a respectable man,' she said softly.

'Yet he's living with you, with a sixty-year-old woman? So does he cheat on you?'

'Possibly,' whispered Gladys, her heart aching with sudden, fierce pain.

'Well, anyway, that's none of my business. Let's get back to me. You imagine nothing else you could offer me apart from money and your belated affection? But what if I were ambitious? What if I weren't happy with the official status you gave me? The natural son of Martial Martin, a former butler, whom he recognised after the fact?'

'It's too late to fix that.'

'Do you think so? We'd have to see about that . . .'

'She's shaking, the old thing,' he thought, enjoying the feeling immensely, 'But then again, who knows?'

At that very moment, however, it wasn't the hope of a brilliant future or even the joy of revenge that made his wicked heart pound with exquisite delight: it was the satisfaction of knowing that he had played his hand well and come out on top.

'You never thought of me once in the past twenty years, did you?'

'No.'

'I could have starved to death.'

'I told Jeanne to come to me if . . .'

'But you went away, didn't you? You left France?'

'Yes,' said Gladys, 'but I thought I'd be coming back in a few months, I swear to you.'

'And you forgot all about me?'

'Yes.'

'The way you forget about a dog?'

'Oh, I'm begging you,' she said, clasping her hands together. 'Let's not talk about the past. The way you look at me . . . Such hatred . . .'

'Will you introduce me to Aldo Monti?'

'Are you mad? Why?'

'Why not?'

'I can't,' she whispered.

'Are you ashamed of me?'

'I'm ashamed of what I did,' she said, instinctively coming up with a lie she thought would appease him.

But he just shook his head and smiled. 'Is that the only reason? Then I absolve you. And who wouldn't understand that you might wish to keep your daughter's mistake a secret?'

'It's exactly because of that, that's why I can't . . . It hurts me, Bernard.'

She broke off when she heard him laughing. And his harsh laughter was followed by a soft voice.

'Come on now, you can stop pretending. You forget that I knew Jeanne and that you can keep no secrets from a chambermaid. You're afraid to admit how old you are and that's all there is to it.'

Blood rushed to Gladys's powdered cheeks, but all she said was, 'My lover is more important to me than anything.'

'Your lover? At your age? You should be ashamed to use the word!'

'I love him. And if I hold on to him, it's not because of virtue or fine feelings. You can't understand that yet. You're still a child. He stays with me because I'm a woman who still looks young and beautiful, and that flatters his ego. If he knew my age, and more importantly, if he knew how I'd lied, how ashamed I am deep down, and what the misery and decay of old age means to me, he'd leave me. And if he stayed it would be worse, because then I'd think that he wanted my money, and I couldn't stand that, I couldn't. I'd want to die. I want to be loved.'

'Well, then, what do you think you will do?'

'I think that you will understand what's in your own best interest. You have nothing to gain from a scandal. According to the law, I owe you nothing. You have a legally recognised father. Anyway,' she said, shrugging her shoulders and looking weary, 'I don't really know anything about the law. But I'm prepared to give you the only thing I can freely give you: money. Later on, in a few years, or even a few months perhaps, my lover will leave me. Overnight I'll become an old woman. That's always the way it happens,' she murmured. 'Things will be different then. But I won't give up the short time I have, not for anything, not for any feeling of either remorse or obligation!'

He said nothing. He had stood up and walked over to her. He stared at her with intense curiosity. Finally, he whispered, 'You can go now.'

She left.

18

Gladys went downstairs and crossed a wide avenue where the first street lights shone through the reddish autumn mist. She was in the student quarter. Every house, every street belonged to the young. Every face she saw was surrounded by a halo of fog and was poor, gaunt and hungry, but young, so young . . . She looked at them with hatred. Bernard's words weighed heavily in her heart. She could still hear them: 'So does he cheat on you?'

He had asked that question so sincerely, almost naïvely. Does he cheat on you? No one could love you, not you, you're old! She had never ever been jealous: she was so sure of herself and her power. But for the first time in her life she now felt that fear, that despair, that horrid hope . . .

'Does he love me? Did he ever love me? Why hasn't he left me, why? Is it because he wants to get married? Is it the money? Is he faithful to me? Why didn't he come to see me yesterday? Where was he? Who was he with? Why?'

When he held her in his arms, when he closed his eyes

and touched her, was it to increase his own pleasure or so that he didn't have to look at her face? Did her face really convey the illusion of youth?

She stopped right there in the middle of the street, took out a mirror from her handbag and studied her face. Then the thought came to her that if she had done the same thing five years ago . . . only five years ago, a man would surely have smiled at her and whispered, 'Oh yes, very pretty, yes . . .'

No one looked at her. Young men walked by, arm in arm. Gladys passed shabbily dressed young women, a beret tilted over one ear, carrying briefcases full of books. She heard one heavy, ugly girl shout out to her friends, 'They went to the Italian lakes!' She pronounced it 'Eye-talian', the better to stress her mocking and surprise, as if she were thinking, 'How could anyone go to the Italian lakes? What show-offs!' But in spite of herself, an envious sadness crept into her voice and Gladys looked at that poor, fat young girl as if she were a friend, because she too had dreams that would never come true.

She went home. Her heart was pounding deeply, painfully, in her chest. That night she couldn't get to sleep. She anxiously stroked her body.

'But I'm beautiful, I'm beautiful. Where would he find a body more beautiful than mine? I'm not sixty; it isn't true! It's not possible! It's some sort of horrible mistake! Why did I go and see that boy? I haven't given him a thought in twenty years. I should have gone away, moved to the other side of the world. But would Aldo have got a letter? Aldo . . . Does he love me? Where is he right now? Does he love another woman? What do I really know about him? What does anyone know about the man she loves? Perhaps he's laughing at me? Perhaps . . .'

She thought of one of her friends, Jeannine Percier, who was always flirting with Monti.

'If he knew . . . If he were told the truth, they'd make fun of me, the two of them. He'd never forgive me for making him look foolish, never. She'd say: "Poor Gladys. You never suspected; but you can't fool a woman. I always knew she was older than people thought, but even then, for her to be . . . Oh, it's hilarious!"' She, Gladys, ridiculous? Odious, yes, criminal, yes, but not ridiculous! A monster, something horrific, but not that, not a grandmother, an old woman, a hag in love!

'I'll show him that I can still be the favourite, that I still know how to make an entrance,' she thought in a surge of fury. 'Bernard . . . That boy wants revenge through a petty lie. I'm beautiful. Who would ever guess my age? And even if people knew,' she thought, 'there are attractive women of fifty or even older, aren't there? Yes, that's what they think, but everyone makes fun of them, the poor things. If they only knew how people laughed at them. Ah, if Aldo were here now, I'd forget about everything. You can't fake desire. If only he were here,' she thought anxiously, getting out of bed. Her beauty mask kept her face from moving; she ripped it off in a rage. How demeaning! Skin products, secrets, the illusion of youth created only by artificial means. The creams, the make-up, her hair dye, the invisible corset underneath the bathing suit in summer . . .

'All those things are bearable to women who have never experienced what it's like to be truly beautiful, serene, triumphant, but to me?' she thought bitterly. She felt a desperate need to see Aldo, to be reassured.

'I'll go to his house. He'll think I'm mad. I'll test his patience,' she whispered in anguish, 'but I can't bear to be alone tonight. I'm not well. If my life were in danger, I'd go to him. I'll die if I have to suffer like this all night.'

She switched on the light and walked over to the mirror and, for a second, she looked at her reflection in terror, expecting to see an old, defeated woman instead of her own familiar face.

She hurriedly got dressed and left. Monti lived in a ground-floor apartment on a quiet street close by. She walked to his house, hoping that walking quickly along the dark street would calm her pounding heart. Through the slits in the shutters everything was dark. 'He'll be asleep.' She went over to the window and rapped on it gently. No reply.

'He must be fast asleep.'

She called him quietly again. She had come to him this way more than once in the past, but then he had been expecting her. Nothing. She listened closely to see if she could hear anything and suddenly, behind the closed shutters, she heard the muffled sound of the telephone ringing beside Aldo's bed. But Aldo didn't answer. Where was he? And who was calling him? Who, apart from her, had the right to call him at five o'clock in the morning? Where was he? She shook the iron shutters furiously, then stopped, overcome by fear that the concierge or the neighbours might come out. She walked back to the corner of the street and sat down on a bench; it was shrouded in the icy fog of early dawn. Mist hung in the branches of the trees. Every now and then a drop of water ran slowly down the back of her bare neck. The street lamp flickered and went out. It was morning. Greyish light rose from the east. A drunkard passed by, swore at her and disappeared. In this calm, wealthy street with its closed windows, the houses looked dark and mocking.

'Who is it?' she thought. 'I'm such a fool!' She was trembling with rage and despair. 'I'm an idiot! A stupid fool! He's cheating on me! And I didn't even see it, never suspected a thing! Who is she? I'd really rather not know,' she thought, feeling cowardly.

But in her heart the feverish question persisted: 'Who is she?'

It was like a wound that you want to rip from your flesh, and too bad if it kills you . . .

'I'll stay here all day long,' she thought in blind rage, 'and then I'll know. He wouldn't dare lie to me.'

Then she was overcome by wild hope.

'Maybe I didn't knock loudly enough. He might be fast asleep, who knows? But the phone ringing . . . I must have imagined that. Who would call him in the middle of the night? I must have been dreaming.'

She hurried over to the window again, grabbed hold of the shutters, shook them with her anxious, weak little hands and called out his name. Her only reply was the worried barking of a dog.

'Jerry?' she called softly. 'Is that you, Jerry?'

The dog recognised her voice, barked again and whined.

'Are you all alone, too?' she whispered in despair. 'Did he leave you all alone as well, my poor Jerry?'

Finally, she saw a taxi come down the empty street and

stop in front of the house. She recognised Monti through the window; there was a woman sitting next to him whom he helped out of the cab. It was Jeannine Percier. She remembered that Jeannine's husband was away for a week and wouldn't get back until the following day. They had spent the evening together. He was wearing a dinner jacket and she could see that Jeannine wasn't wearing a hat. They were going into Aldo's house, as she had done so many times before, to finish the evening properly.

She wanted to rush over, but immediately stopped herself. 'How I must look . . .' she thought. How haggard her face must be after such a night. She had no right to cry, to let anyone see her pain. It was fine for young people to allow tears to run down their faces: it was like rain running down a flower. Jeannine could cry. Jeannine wasn't even thirty. Her tears would make Monti feel tenderness towards her. But she, Gladys, couldn't forget that tears made her make-up run down her cheeks.

She watched them go inside the house and close the door behind them. For a long time she sat on the bench, clasping her bare, frozen hands over her trembling mouth and watching the house. She saw the light come on through the slits in the shutters, then go out. She went home.

19

In the weeks that followed Gladys went back to see Bernard several times; she felt a strange sense of peace in his miserable room, the only place on earth where she had nothing left to fear, or to hide. It was only with him that she could finally allow herself to look like an old, tired woman, where she could let her body slump and relax her neck: she normally held her head up very straight to hide the crease in her neck beneath her pearl necklace. She had asked to meet Bernard's mistress. She was a young woman with fine, angular features and brown hair cut in a fringe that fell forward over her forehead. Her deep, perceptive eyes did not laugh, even when she did; they remained dark and serious, but at other times, when she seemed sad or lost in a dream, they sparkled mockingly. She was called Laurette Pellegrain. She owned nothing in the world except a beige wool suit, a beret and a flowered cotton blouse that she wore even when it was bitterly cold, washing it in the evening and putting it back on the next day. She was one of those young women from Montparnasse whose background and real name were rarely known and who seemed to live on coffee and croissants, a girl whom no one found interesting and who disappeared one fine day as suddenly as she had arrived. Gladys quickly realised that it was for Laurette that Bernard had come to find her: to get Laurette some money.

That day, Gladys stayed with them for a long time, barely speaking, watching the rain run down the windows. Laurette was coughing; it was a deep, painful cough that seemed to rip through her chest.

'Madame,' Bernard said finally, 'this young woman needs to go to Switzerland. Could you help us? I want to find a job,' he added, lowering his head.

'But why, Bernard? I'm here, and . . .'

'I don't want to ask you for money,' he said angrily. 'Don't you understand? Not that. I want to earn my living.'

'All right,' she said with the naïvety of a rich woman. 'That can't be so difficult, can it?'

'That's what you think, is it?' he scoffed. 'What year do you think this is? What dream world are you living in? You'd think you'd fallen asleep before the war and still hadn't woken up; it's incredible!'

'I'll give you all the money you need, Bernard, but apart from that, what can I possibly do?'

'You have friends, acquaintances . . . I know that you know Percier, the Minister.'

'No,' she murmured, 'no, not that. It's impossible. Be content with what I'm offering you.'

She sat up taller, nervous, anxious; the evening rejuvenated her, sent her running to Monti, covered her in the illusion of youth. She threw a cheque down on the table and left.

'She'll be back,' said Laurette, smiling.

She went over to Bernard, looked at him with the perceptiveness that was her most outstanding feature and asked, 'Is that woman your mother?'

'Why? Does she look like me?'

'You both have a murderous look in your eyes, did you know that?' she said, gesturing as she spoke, as she normally did. 'Those murderous eyes that Fragonard so cruelly gives his women . . .'

'Oh, no, Laure, don't talk like that,' he said, looking at her affectionately. 'You sound like an educated tart and there's nothing worse.'

'Yes, my darling,' she murmured, smiling, but without listening to him.

He held her tightly in a fierce embrace. 'You'll go, Laurette, you'll get well . . .'

'Of course I will,' she said softly, stroking his forehead gently with her thin fingers. 'I'll come back. I won't die. You see, if I died now, my life would be like this,' she said, tracing a circle in the air with the tip of her finger, 'it would be perfect, logical destiny. But life is never like that, it's like this,' she said, tracing a broken line with ups and downs that vanished into space, 'or even like this, a question mark . . .'

'Just come back, come back and you'll see, I'll make that woman pay until she's completely drained; she won't have a single drop of blood left in her. Do you want to know her name? It's Jezebel. You don't understand, but it doesn't matter. I don't know anything about you either, but I love you. How I love you, Laure. When you come back, I'll buy you beautiful clothes, jewellery, and all with Jezebel's money. You'll see, my love, you'll see . . .'

Laurette left with her half-empty suitcase full of books, wearing no hat, as usual, holding her beret in her hand, shivering slightly from the cold in her beige wool suit. She set off for Switzerland, where so many before her had gone to be cured.

20

Bernard received two brief little letters from Switzerland made up of short sentences that seemed breathless, then nothing. He knew that Laurette was going to die; every day he expected to hear news of her death. His despair was like him: bitter, bleak and full of venom. He had terrible toothache; he stopped shaving; he didn't open a book; he threw himself down on his bed fully dressed and slept until evening. He woke up when night fell, for he took painful pleasure in the terrible dawns of Paris. He didn't have the strength to leave his shabby room. Where would he go? He found solitude everywhere, sadness, anxiety and cruel boredom lay in wait for him everywhere. He waited until the flame on the gaslight in the street cast the shadow of the shutters on to the dark wall. Then he would stare in silence at the light. Every now and again its soft greenish glow blocked out all his thoughts; it flowed like a soothing balm, deep into his heart. The rain fell, heavy and cold. Laure . . . He pictured her as if she were already dead. She was a private young woman, he thought, unassuming, fragile, with a beautiful body. She had a lively, melancholy spirit, a kind of disheartened grace. Strange

despair took hold of Bernard, a bitter, silent, cold sadness
that was like his own heart. At night he went from café
to café. When he was drinking he forgot about his mistress,
or, at least, he didn't think of her in such cruel detail. But
even in the depths of his drunkenness he missed Laure's
presence; he felt a void, mournful hunger, bleak weariness.

Stretched out on his bed, his thin body shivering beneath
the old cardigan that no one mended any more, a dish
heaped with oranges at his side, watching the rain run
down the windows until he became mesmerised, numbed
by it, to stop himself worrying about death, to avoid
sinking into despair, he forced himself to think about
Gladys, to rekindle in his heart his hatred of Gladys.

'She won't come, not she, no chance of that. I could
drop dead and she wouldn't give me a thought. The only
blood relative I have and yet . . .'

He gave a low moan.

'Laure . . .'

He felt tears welling up in his eyes and was ashamed.
He turned over in bed, furiously crumpling the sheets and
burying his head deep into the yellowed pillow that smelled
musty, like everything in his sordid lodgings.

'Laurette . . . my poor girl . . . You're done for. And to
think that with Jezebel's money I could have bought you
dresses, chocolates . . . You could have had at least some
good times, my poor darling. Well, you won't even have
that . . . not even that . . .'

He was ashamed to be so weak and so in love; he tried
to think, 'Well, there's nothing I can do. Someone else will
come along . . .'

But then immediately: 'Just let her get better, let her

come back, I'll suck the life out of Jezebel, I'll take everything she has. I'll make her suffer, I'll make her curse the day she was born.'

In his mind he had created a strange link between his mistress and the woman he called Jezebel.

'A twenty-year-old girl who is going to die without ever having had even five minutes of happiness on this earth, and that mad old woman with her diamonds who still allows herself to be in love, to be jealous! Hell, it's grotesque. I'd like to murder her,' he sometimes thought. 'What could they do to me? Nothing! Gentlemen of the jury! She was my grandmother. She abandoned me, rejected me, robbed me of what was rightfully mine. I avenged myself. "But she gave you money, my boy!"

'Ah, I have a fever,' he murmured. 'What wouldn't she give for me to catch a good dose of typhoid or Laure's tuberculosis so I might join my mother in a better place! I must really make her worry,' he thought, cheering up. 'All the same, what rotten luck. Everything was against me! I could have died a thousand times! But no, I'm still here. That's certainly some consolation, but it's not enough! No, by God, it's not enough!'

On Christmas Eve he learned that Laurette had died. He decided to go and tell his mistress's parents. He had discovered their address while sorting through some old letters Laure had left in a drawer.

He arrived at a quiet, wealthy apartment; an old dried-up woman with white hair and wearing mourning clothes and a jet necklace asked him to come in. She was Laure's mother; he first told her that Laure had been ill and was receiving treatment in Leysin.

'It had to end like that,' she replied, crying. 'You say she's in Leysin? But that must be terribly expensive. Children are ungrateful things. She left me. She brought me disgrace. What can I do?' she said, wiping her eyes with a handkerchief with black edging, as her jet beads quivered against her chest. 'I lost my husband six months ago. He left me with no money. Tell Laure she must be very frugal. I know my daughter: perfume, make-up, silk stockings. She must be considerate to me. I could send her five hundred francs a month, if I deprive myself of everything. Not a single letter, not a word to her mother in five years, but naturally, as soon as anyone needs something, they turn to their family. I'll send her five hundred francs a month, Monsieur.'

'There's no point,' said Bernard harshly. 'One payment will be enough to bury her. She died yesterday.'

He walked out. It was raining. The night was thick with icy fog. He walked straight ahead, almost without thinking. He went into one bistro, then another. First to the Frégate, opposite the quayside, where you could see shadows reflected in the dark water. Then to a little café on the Ile Saint Louis, where the antique carved beams were lit up by hissing gaslight, then to the Ludo, thick with dust, grime and chalk . . .

Then he went back to Montparnasse. He had another drink, and ran into a friend. 'Laure's dead,' he told him.

'Poor girl. She was barely twenty. Do you want another drink?'

He drank it and left almost immediately to escape into the dark streets; the red lights of the bistro turned the mud the colour of blood. He went to the Dôme and sat on the terrace. He felt a need to tell the world that his mistress had died.

'It's not possible!' they all exclaimed, immediately adding, 'She didn't look very strong . . .'

'How old was she? Twenty, right?' someone asked.

And when they heard her age, so similar to their own, they all fell silent. Bernard kept drinking, looking at the familiar faces through the smoke and feeling dark anger rise within his heart.

For a long time he dragged himself from one café to another.

He headed in the direction of the Seine. He was drunk; his head was hot and his mind blank. He listened to the sound of the rain on the pavement. He walked towards the Bois, towards Gladys's house; he felt a desperate, heinous need to see Gladys.

'I'm going home. I've got to go home,' he said over and over again. 'I've got to get some sleep.'

But in spite of himself his legs dragged him towards Gladys.

He thought about Laure's mother, that old, half-dead woman with her spectacles, her jet necklace, her straw bag, her embroidered cushions, who hoarded her money so it would last a few more miserable years.

'Dirty old hags,' he thought, clenching his fists.

His feeling of hatred encompassed Gladys, Laure's mother and everyone who clung on to their status, their money, their happiness, leaving their children nothing but despair, poverty and death.

As he got closer to Auteuil, the cafés became fewer and poorer. Some men were playing cards. In one of them he listened for a long time to an old player piano that had some of its keys missing.

He thought of the first time he'd met Laure; she was sitting in front of a brazier that cast her in a reddish light; she wore no hat and had a red woollen cravat round her neck; he could picture her pale, delicate features and the look in her eyes.

'There was something about her . . . something I never managed to reach in her, something she never managed to reach in herself . . . a kind of poetry . . .'

He tried to picture his own mother but couldn't imagine what she'd looked like. He forgot that she would have been forty had she lived. He saw her as if she were a sister, as young as he and Laure.

'You poor things, you're dead. You're down there, in the darkness, and they all laugh, dance, pamper themselves. I want to grab Jezebel by the shoulders and shake her, shake her, shake her,' he thought in a rage, 'shake her until her painted mask drops off. Oh, how I hate her. It's all her fault! And it's not just the fact that she's alive. What's going to happen to me? I have a thousand acquaintances and not one friend, not one relative. I want to work. Not study. I'm sick of it. My hands hurt from doing nothing but open books. Work . . . In the métro, in the food market at Les Halles, anywhere. And do you think it's easy in these times of financial crisis, my boy? I should have been a manual worker. Mama Berthe shouldn't have tried to make me into a gentleman. Some days I feel I have a grudge against everything on this earth, God forgive me,' he thought with tenderness and remorse. 'Ah, I'm thirsty . . .'

He went into a café that was open, on the corner of the quayside; he drank outside, in the rain, barely sheltered beneath a canvas awning that flapped in the wind. He was shivering from the cold.

'Any lowly job would save me. Banging in a nail or fitting planks, then falling asleep at night. One year of such a life, getting drunk every Sunday, and I'd forget Laure. After all, I'm twenty. I don't want to die of a broken heart. I don't want to,' he said again with an echo of defiance at an invisible god. 'Yes, but . . . Jezebel's money . . . Money that came to her so easily. Women like her corrupt everything they touch.'

He walked all night. Rain ran down his face and fell with a murmur, a whisper, a patter on to a city that seemed deserted. Mist rose from the street. He half closed his eyes as he walked, tripped over the edge of the pavement like a blind man.

'I'll tell Jezebel . . .' he thought. 'Oh, she'll remember this night. It feels so good to make someone else suffer. What is she doing now? Has she forgotten me? Well, I'll soon make her remember who I am! Where is she?'

He looked at the windows of her house, dark and closed.

'On Christmas Eve, Jezebel is surely out dancing somewhere, if she's not making love at home. She's dancing and having fun. That old woman, that ghoul, that monster! But no, why say such things? She looks young. But she's old, old, old, an old witch,' he said over and over again in bleak delirium. 'I'll make her remember tonight! I want to see tears streaming down her face . . .'

He leaned against the carriage entrance of a house and stood there, watching the rain fall.

21

Meanwhile, Gladys, the Perciers and Monti were dancing at Chez Florence. The evening was a kind of 'fight to the bitter end' between Jeannine and herself: she sensed intangible warning signs that made her feel she was losing the war, that Monti preferred Jeannine to her. Jeannine was like a delicate little vulture; she had a narrow, hooked nose, wide, anxious, bright eyes that continually blinked beneath her pale round eyelids, and dark hair that was as straight and shiny as feathers. That night, she wore her hair in that season's fashionable style: swept into two wings that met at the top of her head to form a kind of turban. She never got tired; she was one of those women who have muscles of steel beneath a delicate frame. She had guessed Gladys's secret weakness: her age. She loved Monti, but more importantly, she loved the glory of having stolen Gladys Eysenach's lover.

She wanted to crush her rival who was weaker but more beautiful, and Gladys, pale and determined, accepted the challenge. If she saw Jeannine was drinking, she drank. If she saw Jeannine dancing, she danced, even though it had become painful for her even to stand. Jealousy tormented her heart. She would have died just to have Monti smile at her or look at her with desire. She felt an almost visceral thrill when she looked at Jeannine. She thought of the gun she had bought: it was still in her handbag, within reach. She talked, laughed, willed herself to be beautiful, the way you whip a tired animal, and Monti felt cruel pleasure as he alternated between the two women, holding first one, then the other close to him and feeling them tremble in his arms.

It had been a long time since Gladys had danced this way, hour after hour, tirelessly, amid the smoke, in the darkness, with faces whirling around her. Her body felt as if it were made of thousands of painful little bones.

'Keep going,' she thought in a rage, 'dance, smile! You have to look carefree, beautiful, young! You have to be attractive, more attractive. Attractive to all these men, so he can see it, so he gets jealous.'

That night she, who had never worn any jewellery apart from a long strand of pearls, had covered her arms and neck in diamonds, for Jeannine didn't own anything as beautiful. She had to be noticed at all costs and it wouldn't occur to her lover to wonder why every man's eyes were on her, whether they were admiring her jewels or herself.

She had to look beautiful, even at five o'clock in the morning, she had to make sure her wrinkles didn't show through her make-up, nor the death mask that lies beneath the heavily made-up faces of old women. Never a moment of relaxation or weariness. Never admit to being weaker. Dance, drink, dance some more. Force the legs and body of a sixty-year-old to keep going and refuse to grow weary. Hold your back straight: it was bare, smooth, powdered a pale ochre colour, as soft as satin, but each and every muscle screamed in pain. Resist shivering when a cold gust of wind rushed in through the door or an open window.

The two women squared up to each other, smiling.

'Darling, do be careful. You'll catch cold . . .'

'How ridiculous! I never get ill or tired.'

'That's true, isn't it?' Jeannine said quietly. 'You must find my generation quite pathetic.'

Gladys could feel her knees shaking; she stood up straighter and thought, 'Keep going, come on, move, you old carcass. Do as I say.'

She smiled and listened in terror to the wheezing from her heavy heart.

Then, by sheer force of will, she ended up not only winning over herself, but triumphing over Jeannine as well; her legs found their former lightness, rhythm and speed; her breathing grew calmer. She now danced with the divine ease she'd had when she was twenty. She smiled, partly opening her beautiful lips. She looked in the mirrors to see the reflection of her white dress, her dyed hair, which she had plaited and wound round the top of her head like a crown, just as she had in the past.

Four o'clock, five o'clock in the morning . . . Bernard waited in the rain. Gladys danced.

But then a group of young men and women came in, slightly drunk and noisy. The young women wore their hair down, loose and flowing; their make-up, so exquisite on their young faces, seemed to merge with their fresh, smooth skin. Secretly, Gladys looked at herself in the mirror and could see her ravaged features peering through her mask of make-up. But she got up, danced again, pressed herself against Monti. Her tired eyes, burning with weariness, closed, in spite of herself.

Jeannine, too, was beginning to show signs of weariness. She was thirty years younger, but not so well protected by her beauty, which was not as perfect as Gladys's. Around them people laughed, keeping score. A battle.

Gladys looked happy and triumphant in the end, but she was obsessed by one thought. Everything reminded her of how old she was; everything brought back memories of the past. She talked and smiled, but deep inside, her obsession slithered through her as slowly as a snake. She wouldn't give up the fight, though; her whole body trembled with the kind of nervous tension that takes hold of people whose will to live is too strong: ravaged, barely breathing, they refuse to die. For Gladys it was tragically impossible to admit defeat.

The other people in the room saw only a woman whose age was impossible to tell, like all the women in Paris who were over forty. Beneath the lights, with her make-up and jewellery, she looked beautiful, but it was a fragile kind of beauty, anxious and pathetic, and standing in the doorway in the early morning light, she seemed to drop her mask, just like all the other older women.

All her effort, all her weariness, her battles, anguish and triumphs came down to a single question asked by one indifferent young man to another as he started up his car: 'Gladys Eysenach? She still looks good. Is she easy?'

22

Bernard waited. He didn't mind the cold. He took pleasure in feeling the wind bite at his cheeks. Paris was filled with the damp, dank smell of marsh water. His mind was a blank. He stared at Gladys's dark windows in the empty street.

Finally he saw the car. It was lit up inside and he recognised Gladys's delicate, blonde little head and her ermine coat.

Her existence aroused a feeling of outrage in Bernard. 'She's laughing,' he thought, clenching his teeth. 'She's dancing and having a good time. But why? She's old, that's what she is, and she doesn't have the right to anything any more . . .'

Bernard reached for the car door, then slipped back into the shadows. Either Monti didn't see him or thought he was some beggar wandering about, hoping for a handout.

But Gladys recognised him at once. Bernard saw her lean in towards Monti; he heard her tell her lover he wasn't to get out. Bernard followed Gladys to her door. She looked at him for a moment without saying a word, terrified by the wave of hatred she felt rushing from her heart. 'Go away!' she whispered at last.

'I want to talk to you. Let me come in.'

'You're mad! Go away!'

The hatred she had tried to stifle, to disguise in all sorts of ways, had risen to the surface, pure and crystal clear; she detested Bernard's voice, the hungry look in his eyes, his sarcastic little laugh; she felt the kind of hatred towards him that you only feel as completely, blindly, cruelly as when it is aimed at a member of your own family.

'I advise you to let me come in,' he said, grabbing her hand.

'Let go of me, stop it! The servants are inside . . .'

Nevertheless, he went in after her. The entrance hall was empty. Bernard looked at the painted walls; a lamp lit up the staircase. He followed Gladys into a dark room. She sat down; her legs were shaking and she held her head like horses do at the end of a race; her entire body was overcome by the excessive stiffness that is a result of terrible over-exertion.

She switched on a lamp draped in pink cloth that sat on her dressing table and automatically raised the collar of her coat to hide the damage to her features caused by her long night. He walked towards her hesitantly; he felt drunk and half asleep, as if in a waking nightmare. They stared at each other for a moment without speaking, both terrified and full of hatred, and for the two of them their intoxication and exhaustion formed a kind of fog, the suffocating stupor you feel in dreams.

Finally she spoke, forcing her voice to sound quiet and

sweet, devoid of any hint of aversion or anxiety. 'What's wrong, my boy? What is it you want from me?'

'I called you the day before yesterday. I called you yesterday. I wrote to you. It seems to me that you're not afraid of me any more, Grandmother dear.'

He felt joy at seeing her go white again and stiffen, as if she were being whipped.

She looked at him nervously. 'You're drunk. Why have you come to torment me? I've helped you as best I could. I've done everything I could to show my sympathy for you.'

'Sympathy?' he said, shrugging his shoulders. 'Fear, yes, but then again, it's probably better this way. I don't need your sympathy.'

'I know,' she said with strange bitterness, 'all you need is my money.'

'Are you reproaching me for not having found you out of a need for affection? That would really be the height of hypocrisy.'

Wearily she closed her eyes. 'What do you want from me? Just tell me and go away! What do you want from me?' she said again, stamping her foot on the parquet floor in one of her sudden angry fits of temper that erupted only rarely and contorted her pale, anxious face. 'You want money, of course? Fine, just tell me how much and then go away.'

He shook his head. 'I don't need your money any more. Did you think that all you had to do was throw money at me and I'd keep quiet, be subdued, taken in by you? How right people are when they say you never really know your family!'

'Well, then, what do you want?' she murmured. 'To make me suffer, I assume, simply to make me suffer? That's it, isn't it?'

They looked at each other for a long time without speaking.

'Yes,' he finally admitted, looking away; his voice was low and passionate. 'Listen, I don't want to live the way I do any more. I want you to use your contacts, your reputation, your friends, to make up a little for the monstrous injustice you have done me. I don't want to remain the son of Martial Martin. I'm not Bernard Martin. Or, at least, if I keep the name Bernard Martin, I don't want it associated with some penniless waif. I'm willing to work, I'm strong and intelligent. Listen: this is what I want from you. You will give me a letter of recommendation right now for your friend Percier, so that he gives me a job, the lowliest little clerical job he likes, I don't care. I need help getting started, do you understand?'

Gladys looked at him with the kind of panic and fear that clouds reason: the confusion in her heart was so great that she barely heard the last thing Bernard said. Percier ... Jeannine's husband ... What if Jeannine found out, my God!

'No,' she said.

'Why?'

'I can't. Not Percier. Besides, he wouldn't listen to me. This isn't the right time to discuss business,' she whispered, terrified. 'I can't!'

'Why?'

'It's impossible!'

'So you're refusing?' he shouted, sensing in the way she resisted that he had found some secret weakness, some wound he could open, deepen, make bleed at will.

'Bernard, that's enough. Go away! We'll talk tomorrow.'

'Why? I've waited for you long enough. I've suffered long enough. Now it's your turn. Are you expecting someone, perhaps? Well, can you imagine anything funnier than us meeting like this? Could anything be more wonderful? More unexpected? More comical? What do you think?' he said again in a rage. 'The door opens and the lover enters. "Madame! Who is this young man? Your lover, without a doubt?" No, not her lover, her grandson!' Oh, how exquisite. Your face. Just look at yourself in the mirror! Now you really do look like a grandmother. You couldn't hide your age if you tried. Look, look,' he said, holding a mirror in front of her face. 'Look at the bags under your eyes that show through the make-up. You're old! You're an old, old woman,' he said again and again, beside himself. 'How I hate you!'

She grabbed the mirror from his trembling hands, studied her face for a long time, opening wide her despairing eyes. 'Bernard, sometimes I think you hate me less for the past than for the present. Why? What harm can it do you that I'm still a real woman, that I have a lover?'

'It disgusts me,' he murmured.

'Why? Bernard, why? You're young. You love your mistress. How can you not understand that I am in love, that I'd give my life to be loved? You look at my dresses, my furs, my jewellery and you want to take them away from me and give them to Laurette. I'd happily give them away. If you only knew how much I've suffered today! My lover . . .'

'Shut up! There are certain words you have no right to say. They're monstrous coming from your mouth . . . unnatural. You're sixty years old, you're an old woman. Love, lovers, happiness, such things are not meant for you. You old people should be content with the things we can't take away from you,' he said in a fury, thinking of Laure's mother. 'Keep your money, keep your status, keep your reputation, but those other things, those at least were meant for us. They were ours, ours! Who gave you the right to take them? *You*, in love? You're a poor old woman who's mad,' he said with a bitter laugh, 'but then, if that's the way it is, if you have the *right* to love and be loved, why are you and women like you so afraid of having anyone know how old you are? You'd be less ashamed if you'd committed some crime. You'd happily see me dead if that could help you hide your age. I hate you because you're old and I'm young, and because you're the one who's happy, you, while I'm the one who should have been happy, because I'm young. You've stolen that from me. Besides, you hate me too. But you don't have the courage to say it to my face. You call me "my boy". You smile grotesquely with a mouth that would actually prefer to snap at me!'

'Why should I love you?' said Gladys quietly. 'What are you to me? I'm not the one who brought you into this world. You're not my son. It doesn't make any difference to me that we're related. That's the kind of thing men consider important. I don't know you. You're a stranger to me. There's only one thing that matters to me and that's my lover.'

'That makes me want to die laughing,' said Bernard.

But she continued without listening to him, 'He means everything in the world to me, because if he left me there would be no one left in my life, and a life in which no one loves you, no one desires you, is cold, dead, the life of an old woman, and when all is said and done, to me, it's worse than death.'

'How dare you speak of love? A woman's love? While I, your child . . .'

What am I saying, he thought in despair, but he sensed that he was right.

'You think you've triumphed over age. But it's there, within you. You might show off your supple body and a back that looks like a young woman's, you can dye your hair, go out dancing, but your soul is old. It's worse than that. It's corrupt. There's the foul scent of death about you.'

'Shut up! Leave me alone! You're either drunk or mad. What did I ever do to you? I'm not taking anything away from you. Every human being wants his share of happiness. What have I done that's so wrong? I'm free. My life . . .'

'Your life . . . But why should your life be important? You've had your share of life! You're the one who's always been happy, and I . . . Oh, how I want to make you suffer. I can't understand why I don't just kill you. Would anyone blame me? Yes, of course they would, of course. I'd have committed matricide, but it would be the only time I'd be allowed to say I was related to you and that you were my grandmother. No, no, it would be more satisfying if I just told the truth to your lover . . .'

'Listen to me. What good would it do you to tell the

truth? Well? You would have killed me, that's true. But you'd have no more support, no more money.'

'What difference do you think your money makes to me? Laure died yesterday. And as for your support, as you call it, I know only too well that you'll never give me any. Well, then? At least I would have the satisfaction of taking away your illusions, Grandmother! For now it's your turn to listen to me, because I'm going to tell you what's going to happen. I'm going to tell your lover that you're an old woman, that you're sixty,' he said, savouring the words, 'and he'll stay with you. He'll take it all on. Because it's not you he loves, it's your money. And that way, you poor madwoman, that way, you'll see . . .'

He stopped short. The telephone was ringing. He laughed quietly.

'Is that him? Is that your crazy lover? Well, well, this is going to be fun.'

'No, Bernard!'

'But yes! I couldn't have dreamed of anything better! "Is that Count Monti? This is Bernard Martin." A man at his mistress's house! At this hour? "Oh, not really a man. A boy. Almost your child. Her grand . . ."'

'Bernard!' She lunged at him.

He blocked the telephone with his body, spoke softly, lovingly, choosing his words. "The grandson of your mistress! The grandson of the beautiful Gladys Eysenach!"'

'Bernard, don't answer it! Bernard, don't tell him! I haven't done anything to you! Please . . . Please forgive me, Bernard! Forgive me! You'll see, you'll be rich, happy,' she shouted, trying to drown out the sound of the telephone that kept on ringing and that Bernard was holding in his hands. 'Put the phone down!'

He started to reach for the receiver. Then she pulled out the gun, the gun she had thought of every night for the past month.

He looked at her with a strange, scornful twitching of his lips. She fired. He dropped the telephone; his face had suddenly changed: it was soft and surprised. He fell to the floor, dragging the insistent telephone with him.

She saw the bewildered, silent look of death spread over his features. Before crying out, before calling for help, before feeling any remorse or despair, a sensation of utter peace filled her heart. The telephone had stopped ringing.